Skulduggery Pleasant

HELL BREAKS LOOSE

DEREK LANDY

Skulduggery Pleasant

HELL BREAKS LOOSE

HarperCollins Children's Books

First published in the United Kingdom by
HarperCollins *Children's Books* in 2023
HarperCollins *Children's Books* is a division of
HarperCollins*Publishers* Ltd
1 London Bridge Street
London SE1 9GF

www.harpercollins.co.uk

HarperCollins*Publishers*
Macken House, 39/40 Mayor Street Upper
Dublin 1, D01 C9W8, Ireland

1

HB ISBN 978-0-00-858573-0
LIMITED EDITION HB ISBN 978-0-00-862294-7
ANZ TPB ISBN 978-000-858603-4
EXP TPB ISBN 978-000-858602-7

Derek Landy asserts the moral right to be
identified as the author of the work

A CIP catalogue record for this title
is available from the British Library

Typeset in Baskerville MT 11/13.5 pt by
Palimpsest Book Production Ltd, Falkirk, Stirlingshire

Printed and bound in the UK using 100% renewable electricity
at CPI Group (UK) Ltd

*This book is dedicated to the thing
with the long arms and the crooked smile
standing behind you*

Italy, 1703

1

The psychic sat on a rock at the edge of camp, his legs folded beneath him, his hands resting on his knees, his eyes closed and his mind open. It was his task to remain alert while the others slept in their tents and in their blankets, safe under his protection. Sentries were not required when you had a Sensitive in your merry band of killers, trained to detect the mind of an enemy moving into range.

But in order to detect such a mind, in order to read its thoughts – dark with malicious intent or otherwise

– those thoughts needed to flicker within the grey folds of an actual physical brain. Skulduggery Pleasant possessed no such thing. His brain had been burned from his skull, along with his eyes and his tongue and his hair and his skin and all the flesh and the muscle beneath. How he moved, how he spoke, how he thought were matters of mystery that not even he, with his vast intellect, had been able to ascertain. Maybe when the war was over, when Mevolent was defeated and the threat had abated, he could devote his time to uncovering the secret of his continued existence, but for now he had devoted his full attention to the fight.

Skulduggery emerged from the darkness without making a sound. He walked up to the psychic, sitting there with his legs folded and his eyes closed and his mind open, and clobbered him about the head with a heavy stick. Once the Sensitive was nothing more than an unresponsive heap, Skulduggery motioned for the others to advance.

As he and the others moved forward, stepping over damp twigs and ducking under the thin branches of olive trees, Ghastly Bespoke couldn't help but be impressed. In the thirteen years since Skulduggery had lost his family and died himself, he had been sinking steadily deeper into a pit of violent nihilism. His humour had become as sharp as the sword he wore on his hip, and as pointed as the lucky knife he often used to cut the throats of sentries and Sensitives. The fact that here he had chosen the relatively benign option of a quick bludgeoning in place of a slit throat indicated to Ghastly that his best friend was perhaps finally ready to climb out of the pit and rejoin his fellow Dead Men in the relative brightness of a moonlit night in Tuscany.

"I'm proud of you," Ghastly whispered when he was near enough.

"I am unable to find my lucky knife," Skulduggery whispered back. "I put it in my lucky sheath and hung it from my lucky belt, but it must have fallen off on the way here."

"That would seem to me unlucky," said Ghastly.

"I have tremendous fondness for that knife. Remember when I killed that goblin with it?"

"A delightful moment, indeed. You still have your sword, though."

Skulduggery grunted and tapped the hilt. "If I try to cut a throat with this, I would take the whole head off.

Widow's Lament is a fine sword, no doubt, but its home is on the battlefield. That is where it sings. My lucky knife had its own song, and it was quieter but no less sweet, like a whisper in a storm."

Ghastly didn't like Skulduggery talking about the songs his blades sang. It was discomfiting.

"All still asleep," Saracen Rue said softly, nodding to the camp as he crept up to them. "The first Teleporter's in the tent closest to the fire, sleeping on his belly with his head turned away from the opening. The second one is in the tent on the far side."

"I shall dispatch the first one," Skulduggery said.

"And I the second," said Hopeless, and vanished into the night.

Skulduggery turned to Saracen. "Could I borrow a small blade?"

Saracen frowned. "What happened to your lucky knife?"

"I lost it."

He handed Skulduggery a knife like any other knife Ghastly had ever seen. "Then you may use my lucky knife. I call it the *Blade of Remembering*."

"Why do you call it that?"

"I forget."

They kept whispering, discussing knives and swords. Ghastly had never named any of his weapons. Naming a sword was like naming a spoon, and Ghastly didn't see the point of naming cutlery. He looked over to the north side of the clearing. Erskine Ravel stood waiting beside a tree, twirling his finger in the air like the sun going round the Earth, and Ghastly nodded. Time was passing.

"We should probably do what we came here to do," Ghastly said.

Skulduggery flipped the *Blade of Remembering* in the air and caught it. "Then let us not tarry on this night of blood-letting," he said, and then he was away, sneaking through the shadows.

Ghastly looked at Saracen. "I didn't know you named your weapons."

"I don't," Saracen replied, "because I am not a crazed madman. I said what I said to make Skulduggery feel somewhat normal. I have been thinking about this, and have reached the conclusion that maybe what is missing from his life is a sense of normality."

Ghastly wasn't so sure. "How normal do you expect him to feel as the world's only living skeleton?"

"The world's only living skeleton *so far*," Saracen said, then shrugged. "Ah, you might be right, my friend. I do think, however, that he is starting to come to terms with what happened. I feel that he has been better able to manage his rage these last few months. There was a time when he would have charged into that camp, roaring invectives and eager for battle. Now look at him, dispatching the Sensitive and the Teleporter first, like a reasonable human being. He didn't even kill this one."

Saracen nudged the unconscious psychic with his boot, and the unconscious psychic sat up, blinking and suddenly not very unconscious at all, and screamed.

"Damn," Saracen said, kicking the Sensitive back into unconsciousness.

There were shouts now from the camp, calls to action, and Ghastly could see figures stumbling out of tents, grabbing swords and axes. A stream of vibrant energy punched through the dark, went sizzling through the treetops to disperse in the night sky, and then Skulduggery came sprinting towards them.

"Run away," he said as he passed, and Ghastly and Saracen bolted after him.

They plunged into the trees and an arrow went whistling by Ghastly's ear. It occurred to him that both Skulduggery and Hopeless must have succeeded in dispatching the Teleporters, or else their enemy would be appearing ahead of them instead of giving chase. So that was some good news.

Skulduggery snapped his fingers, the spark flashing in the dark but not igniting to a fireball, and at the signal Ghastly ducked and spun and crouched behind a tree. Now all Ghastly could hear was the stomping, stumbling footsteps of the soldiers as they crashed through the undergrowth, their impulse to give chase outweighing any consideration of stealth. They didn't need stealth when they had the numbers, after all.

Swinging a sword or an axe in a forest was a futile act at the best of times. Ghastly took his own axe from his belt and laid it gently on the ground. The soldiers had slowed considerably. Even idiots could sense a trap. They stepped cautiously but no less noisily, whispering to each other like players on a stage.

The tip of the sword came first, leading the rest of the blade past the tree Ghastly crouched behind. He waited till he could see the hands gripping the hilt, and then he merely stepped out. He closed his hand round his enemy's and punched the soldier so hard he felt the man's nose break. The soldier squealed and tried to pull his sword free, but Ghastly hit him again, on the chin this time, and the soldier crumpled. Another soldier rushed forward, but his sword chopped at an overhead branch and got stuck there. Ghastly pushed at the open space and the air rippled, and the soldier hit the tree behind him like he'd been launched from a catapult.

Ghastly saw Skulduggery and Saracen spring at the other soldiers and the night was suddenly alive with bursting fireballs and streams of energy. He ducked the swipe of a cudgel and felt ribs break beneath his knuckles. The cudgel fell from the soldier's hands and he scrabbled at his belt for a dagger even as he wheezed and gasped, but Ravel was there, burying his own axe into the soldier's head and then scooping up the fallen cudgel and diving back into the fray.

A soldier collided with Ghastly and they went down, rolling over and over until they hit a tree, the soldier doing his best to put his knife in Ghastly's face the entire time. They rolled back again and Ghastly took the soldier's knife from him and put it through the man's neck. He pushed himself to his feet and watched the violence unfold in the darkness around him, accompanied by loud grunts and curses and little cries of pain.

When it was over, Ghastly found his axe and slid it into his belt. He followed the others back to camp, where Dexter Vex was waiting with a prisoner.

"Everyone, meet Adalbert," said Dexter.

Adalbert, a big man with a long, thin beard, was on his knees, his hands shackled behind his back. His left eye was swelling shut and his lip was bleeding. Dexter's own handsome face was unblemished.

"Adalbert is just about to tell us everything we need to know regarding what's waiting for us in the town ahead."

"No, I'm not," said Adalbert.

"Ah, please?" said Dexter.

"Go to hell," Adalbert said.

Skulduggery stepped forward. "Adalbert, do you know who we are?"

Adalbert sneered. "I know who you are. I know who all of you are. The one who ambushed me is Dexter Vex, killer of women and children. You are the living skeleton. Nefarian Serpine killed your family and then he killed you. Erskine Ravel stands by your side, the only man to walk away from the Battle of Day's End. Yes, I've heard the stories. On your other side is Saracen Rue, who murdered his own brothers and sisters in a fit of rage. Beside him is the scarred man, who was born so ugly his own mother died of fright while giving birth to him."

"My mother is still alive," said Ghastly, frowning.

"That's not what I heard."

"Seeing as you have got most of your facts wrong, what you heard is irrelevant. My mother still lives."

"Unless you can prove otherwise, I don't believe you," Adalbert said. "There are two more of you, but I can't see them. Maybe they're hiding. Are they hiding? I'd heard that the one called Hopeless, the assassin, is a gutless coward who only kills when his victim's back is turned."

"You know what they call us," Skulduggery said.

Adalbert gave a short nod. "They call you the Dead Men."

"Because we undertake what would be suicide missions for anyone else."

"And also because you are dead," said Adalbert, "and the others soon will be." He chuckled.

"But there are seven of us," Skulduggery said. "You only named six. Who is the seventh? Do you know?"

Adalbert's chuckle dried in his mouth. "I know," he said. "I know that you have a monster among you, a monster that would as soon kill any of you as kill me. I know you cannot trust this man because any mage who has chosen that discipline cannot be trusted."

"That's right," Skulduggery said. "Because they are too volatile. Too unpredictable. Too violent and bloodthirsty."

Adalbert swallowed. "Yes."

Anton Shudder and Hopeless joined them in camp and Adalbert paled.

"We don't like to threaten people with Anton's Gist," Ghastly said. "For one thing, he is our friend, and we do not want to treat him as a weapon. For another thing, you are absolutely right: the Gist poses just as much of a threat to us as it does to you. To ask Anton to unleash it is to risk our own bloody, terrifying deaths."

"So we shall look on from back there," said Saracen, pointing behind them.

Adalbert shook his head. "You won't do this. You won't let him kill me. I am unarmed. My hands are shackled and my magic is bound."

"Think over everything you have just said about us," said Skulduggery. "Think over all those things you've heard. Because while you may have got some things wrong – Dexter is not the killer of women and children that you think he is, Hopeless is no coward, and Ghastly's mother is still alive – all those other things are true, more or less. We *are* killers. We *are* ruthless. We will do whatever we need to do to accomplish our mission. And, if that means allowing Shudder's Gist to tear you apart because you will not tell us what we want to know, then so be it. Anton?"

Shudder hesitated, then stepped forward.

"Stop," said Adalbert. "Stop. I'll tell you. I will. I swear. Whatever you want to know."

"We know that Baron Vengeous is in the town ahead," Skulduggery said, "but we do not know why."

Adalbert nodded quickly. "*La Porta dell'Inferno*. That's why we're all here. Mevolent sent him to find out if it was real. If it could be opened."

"The Gate to Hell?" Dexter said. "What is that?"

"A portal to the Faceless Ones' dimension," said Ravel.

"Or that's what it's supposed to be, at any rate. I have heard stories about it, stories going back a hundred years or more. It was known to be in Italy, in Tuscany, but I thought its precise location had been lost."

"It was lost," Adalbert said, "but it is lost no longer. Baron Vengeous discovered it was here, in San Gimignano. They are working on opening it wider. Your time is coming to an end. Soon, the Faceless Ones will burn the mortal infestation from the face of the world."

Skulduggery looked at Ghastly. "Meritorious gathered the Dead Men together and sent us here for this? To stop a race of imaginary gods?"

"Blasphemer," muttered Adalbert.

"Blasphemer, am I?" Skulduggery said, laughing as he hunkered down to look Adalbert in the eyes. "We live in the real world, my deluded friend. The threats we deal with are real: war, poverty, vampires, famine. Are you really so lost, so insecure, that you need to put your faith in stories your parents told you by candlelight?"

"The Faceless Ones strode upon this Earth once and they will do so again."

"We are three years into the eighteenth century, you outrageous buffoon. Please act accordingly."

"Whether or not the Faceless Ones are real is immaterial," Ravel said. "The fact is, the *Porta dell'Inferno* has been located and whatever is on the other side will probably not be good news for us or the world at large. Therefore, closing it forever or simply destroying it would seem to be the best course of action for us to take. Any arguments?"

No one objected, and Skulduggery looked back at Adalbert.

"You said they."

Adalbert did a terrible job at feigning innocence, most likely due to being unaccustomed to the sensation. "Pardon?"

"You said Vengeous found the Gate to Hell, but that 'they' are working on it. Who are they?"

"They," said Adalbert. "Vengeous and his soldiers. People like me."

"If you were referring to people like you, you would have said 'we' are working on it, but you did not. You said 'they'. Who is they, Adalbert?"

"I don't know what you mean. I misspoke. I meant to say 'we'."

"Who is with Vengeous?"

"Nobody."

"Shudder," said Skulduggery, "I'm afraid it is time to unleash your Gist."

"Mevolent!" Adalbert cried. "Mevolent's with him! Mevolent and Serpine! Please don't kill me!"

2

The Dead Men were waiting at the inn for Meritorious to get there, indulging in an elegant dinner of a fine young turkey, a tongue *à la daube*, and a salad of anchovies and lettuce. Dessert consisted of cheese and biscuits, almonds in their shells, and butter churned since their arrival spread over excellent, though expensive, bread. The wine was exquisite, even if the Dead Men drank sparingly. They had seen too many of their friends lost to drunken mistakes over the years, and had no desire to add their own lives to the tally.

Ghastly found himself watching the mortals as their precious moments bled from them. He liked to think that if he, too, was mortal, if he could only expect to live forty or forty-five years, he wouldn't waste what little time he had waiting for a cup of wine or a plate of food to be served to him. He liked to think that he would fill his days with friendship and love and family, and never would he darken his hands with violence.

But Ghastly was a man of contradictions, and he liked to think a lot of things.

Being a sorcerer, knowing that his magic would extend his life to perhaps many hundreds of years, offered him nothing in the way of excuses when it came to how he did spend his days. If he, in all his wisdom, shook his head with sage disapproval at the squalid conduct of the unenlightened masses while, at the same time, filling his hands with sword and fire, then what grand lesson had he, in fact, learned? The answer, he was forced to conclude, was none. He had been gifted by the gods or by nature with long life and power, and he chose to pass his moments mired in war and conflict and killing. In truth, he was no better than the fumbling mortals around him. In truth, he was, perhaps, far worse.

Instead of the family he had once promised himself, he had joined a band of brothers, bonded by blood spilled rather than blood shared. The Dead Men were his family: a group of individuals too damaged to operate as part of a larger whole, but just damaged enough to carve out their own bloody paths.

No children for Ghastly Bespoke. No wife or husband or anything approaching that, not since Anselm, absent now from his life these past seven years. When Skulduggery's family had been murdered, when Ghastly had lost one of his best friends – as well as the child to whom he had served as uncle with his whole heart – Anselm had done his very best to see him through the worst of it. Ghastly had devoted himself to helping Skulduggery, and Anselm had devoted himself to helping Ghastly, which left no one devoting themselves to helping Anselm.

Ghastly didn't blame him, not for one instant, and he appreciated the way Anselm had waited till he had regained his footing before striking out. He had known it was coming for a time before it happened. He had known it since that cold evening when they'd sat by the fire and Anselm had said, "I wish, sometimes, that I could see what it is you're chasing. Then maybe I would have a chance of becoming it."

Ghastly hadn't known how to respond to that, neither the words spoken nor the sadness behind them. But that was the first time either of them acknowledged the existence of a *something* between them: a gap, a wedge, a hesitation. Something that stopped them from fitting together with the snugness they would have needed to survive.

The war had taken its toll on a lot of people over the years and a lot of couples, and it took its toll on Ghastly and Anselm. Which was why Anselm was now somewhere else and why Ghastly was here in Tuscany, waiting to be told who to kill next.

A man staggered into the inn, announced to one and all that there was a cat stuck in a wheel out by the bridge, and staggered out, presumably to spread the news further. No one in the tavern appeared to care, and certainly nobody stirred, until Hopeless gave a little sigh and said, "I'll just be a minute."

He left, and after a moment Ghastly followed him into the afternoon sun. They walked up to the bridge, a bridge countless pilgrims had passed over on the road to Rome. There was an old, overturned wagon beside it.

"What do you think of all this?" Ghastly asked as they walked.

"I don't know," said Hopeless. "I shall have to see the cat to form an opinion."

"I meant about Mevolent being in town."

"Oh." He shrugged.

"That's the sum total of your opinion? A single shrug? We have a chance to end the war."

"We have had chances before," said Hopeless. "Every chance we've had, we have failed to actually end it. Mevolent is still walking around. So is Vengeous and so is Serpine. Sometimes I think the war is going to go on forever."

"You used to be funnier."

"No, I wasn't."

"No," Ghastly agreed, "you weren't."

Skulduggery was undoubtedly the most famous of the Dead Men, and Shudder was definitely the most feared. But Hopeless was by far the deadliest of them all. He'd been a knife in the darkness once upon a time, one of the hidden blades – an assassin without equal. Ghastly had known him for over seventy years, but barely knew him at all. It was as if he wore a different face for different people: when he spoke to Saracen, he was warm; when he spoke to Shudder, he was quiet; when he spoke to Skulduggery, he was cold.

Whenever he spoke to Ghastly, though, he just seemed sad.

They reached the wagon. It lay tilted on one side, due in large part to only having one wheel – the wheel which now had a cat trapped between two collapsed spokes. The animal seemed calm as they approached, but once it noticed them it started struggling.

"Hello, Mr Cat," said Hopeless gently. "I see you have found yourself in a bit of a predicament. How did you manage that, I wonder?"

The cat did not respond, and Hopeless moved towards it slowly. Ghastly stayed where he was.

"I am worried about Skulduggery," Ghastly said, "about what he'll do now that Serpine is so close. What do you think he will do?"

Hopeless crouched by the wheel. The cat tried turning its head to hiss at him, and when that failed it made do with simply hissing. "I think Skulduggery will do what Skulduggery does."

"Which is?"

"Whatever he decides."

"I cannot tell if you think you are being helpful."

Closing one hand firmly around the cat's upper body and ignoring the animal's claws, Hopeless used the other to try to loosen one of the spokes.

"Skulduggery prides himself on his ability to follow logic beyond the point where it makes sense to the rest of us, while at the same time being an unashamed slave to his own darker impulses. He is a contradiction, and he has been for as long as I have known him."

"So you're saying we cannot possibly predict what he is going to do?"

"I'm saying *you* cannot predict what he is going to do."

Hopeless let go of the cat and used both hands to pull the spokes further apart. The old wood strained and creaked. "I know exactly what he is going to do, should the opportunity for immediate revenge present itself."

"And that is?"

"He is going to kill Serpine." One of the spokes

cracked and snapped off, and the cat squirmed free and bolted into the undergrowth beneath the bridge without even a by-your-leave. Hopeless straightened. "Goodbye, Mr Cat."

The cat didn't answer.

Hopeless turned to Ghastly. "I might be wrong, but I do not think I am. Skulduggery is the darkest of us all."

"I thought you were."

"I am the deadliest," Hopeless corrected. "Skulduggery is the most notorious, Shudder is the scariest, and Skulduggery, once again, is the darkest. In case you're wondering, Dexter's the most honest, Saracen's the most charming, Ravel's the most loyal and you are the most decent."

"Ah," said Ghastly, "I'm the boring one."

Hopeless sucked the blood from the scratches on his hand. "I'd prefer to be boring than deadly."

They got back to the tavern. As they retook their seats, Eachan Meritorious strode in. Behind him were three women in long cloaks, wearing cloth masks over their faces. The mortals frowned and muttered at the strangers' appearance, but said nothing.

"Gentlemen," Meritorious said in greeting as he sat.

Saracen frowned. "Grand Mage, I can't help but notice that you do not have the army with you. We are less than half a day's ride from Mevolent himself and you come to taverns without a battalion stationed outside?"

"The army is not coming," Meritorious said. "And I am not staying."

Ghastly leaned forward on his elbows. "You think our information is incorrect?"

"On the contrary," said Meritorious, "I think your information is completely accurate, and I commend you for gathering it. I commend you for every step you have taken along the way, right up to this point. You have done exemplary work."

"Then explain," Skulduggery said from beneath the bandages wrapped round his skull.

"I sent you here to verify if Baron Vengeous was, indeed, in San Gimignano. It appears my information was correct, which is very gratifying to know. If Vengeous were alone, I would send you after him without hesitation. You would capture him and he would face justice for every one of his crimes." The barkeep started to come over, but Meritorious waved him away. "However, in light of these developments, a different plan is needed. You have a new mission."

Dexter nodded gravely. "You want us to assassinate Mevolent."

"Actually, I want you to save him from assassination."

The table went quiet. Then Saracen laughed. Then stopped.

"Oh, God," he said, "you're serious."

Meritorious indicated the women standing behind him. "Allow me to introduce some new friends of ours – the Masked Sisters, followers of the Lady of Darkness. This is Rapture, Zeal and Stone."

The Masked Sisters nodded in turn. Sister Zeal was one of the tallest women Ghastly had ever seen, and he'd seen giants. Her hair was long and the colour of straw. Sister Stone was smaller but still tall, her dark hair tied in braids. They were both strong, with broad shoulders beneath their cloaks. Sister Rapture's hair was blonde and short. She wasn't as tall, and wasn't as broad, but she was obviously in charge.

"Greetings, brothers," she said.

"You follow the ways of the Lady of Darkness," said Shudder. "You are no sisters of ours."

"The Lady of Darkness is a mother to us all," Rapture replied. "She casts her shadow over the world and shields us from the sun. You are our brothers, whether you wish it or not."

"The Masked Sisters came to the Sanctuary with new information," Meritorious said before Shudder could argue. "Their Sensitives had foreseen Mevolent's arrival in Tuscany, and they had foreseen his death."

"By our hand?" Ghastly asked.

"By the hand of an assassin named Strickent Abhor."

"Then we let this assassin kill Mevolent," Skulduggery said. "It is something we have failed to do on multiple occasions ourselves, and now you wish to prevent it?"

"If Mevolent dies by Abhor's hand, catastrophe will follow," said Rapture.

"This entire war is a catastrophe. Let it follow. Mevolent's death will be worth it."

"No," said Meritorious, "it will not. Mevolent is trying to prise wider the Gate to Hell. He thinks it leads to a universe where the Faceless Ones are waiting. He is wrong. It will instead unleash a torrent of magical energy that will devastate this land, that will boil the seas and poison the air for centuries to come."

Ravel narrowed his eyes. "And you would have us stand by and allow Mevolent to proceed with this madness?"

"That is what *would* happen," Rapture said, "if Mevolent didn't realise his mistake at the last possible moment, and use his considerable power to reseal the Gate to Hell forever. Strickent Abhor, our Sensitives tell us, will kill Mevolent before he comes to this realisation. Once he is dead, the Gate will remain open, and open wider, and the world will be cracked in two."

"How accurate are your Sensitives?" Hopeless asked.

"Very," said Rapture.

"Our own Sensitives have confirmed it," Meritorious said.

Ghastly pushed his tankard away. He'd barely drunk from it. "And who has sent this assassin?"

"We do not know," Rapture answered.

"Do we have any information that hasn't been gleaned from psychics and dreamers?"

"You doubt what the Sensitives see?"

"I have been fighting in this war long enough, Sister Rapture. On more than one occasion, I have been sent into battle purely on the words of a Sensitive, and I have trusted them as far as I am able. But what they foresee rarely comes true. Knowledge of the future changes the future – that is the first rule of *seeing* the future."

From the way Rapture's mask moved, Ghastly could tell she was smiling a little. "This is true, undoubtedly. But then would not the second rule of seeing the future be that if you fail to act on what has been glimpsed, you are simply allowing it to happen? We can second-guess fate every moment of every day for the rest of our lives, but the truth is that we must do what we can when faced with a choice. That is all we can ever do."

Skulduggery turned to Meritorious. "If the psychics are correct, and we sneak into San Gimignano and protect our enemy from this assassin, what happens afterwards?"

Meritorious shrugged. "Once Mevolent has sealed the Gate to Hell, you may do what you wish."

"And did the psychics foresee us killing Mevolent once this is over?"

"They did not."

"I did not think so. You are asking us to save his life."

"No, Skulduggery, I ask no such thing. Instead, I

command it. You will protect him, and the Masked Sisters will help you. Sister Stone is a Sensitive and can shield the thoughts of the group from Mevolent's people. If you do not consider yourself able to carry out my orders, tell me now and I will have you replaced. If it is too difficult a task for you, for any of you, for the Dead Men as a whole, tell me now. There are other soldiers who will do what needs to be done."

"No one is asking to be replaced," said Hopeless.

"Protecting Mevolent means protecting Baron Vengeous, too – and Nefarian Serpine. They must be allowed to investigate *La Porta dell'Inferno* and then seal it once they realise what it is. If you do not think you can do that, I will understand."

"We can do it," said Ghastly. "Skulduggery, tell him."

"We can protect Mevolent and Vengeous," said Skulduggery.

"And Serpine?"

"Serpine, too," Skulduggery said. "Of course."

The Dead Men and the Masked Sisters rode towards the towers of San Gimignano, following the road between farmland and vineyards and cypress groves.

The warm air brought with it hints of saffron and something Ghastly couldn't identify. They passed people on horseback or in carts and received wary looks from each and every one of them – the Sisters for their hidden faces, Ghastly for his scars, and Skulduggery for his head covered in bandages.

The town ramparts rose from the rolling hills, but it was the towers that caught the attention – dozens of them dotting the skyline, a sign of wealthy families vying for influence. On their approach to Tuscany, the Dead Men had passed plenty of miserable hovels, little more than roofs of planks that looked, from a distance, like tents. Entire families slept upon palliasses, if they even had any, surviving on chestnuts and macaroni. Contrasting that with the opulence on display here was a somewhat jarring sensation.

To the west of San Gimignano were the remains of a fort, to the north a church, in the middle the cathedral. They left their horses outside the walls and joined the flow of people travelling through the town's narrow veins and arteries, breathing in the familiar smells of civilisation. The houses were flat-roofed, with either a low parapet round the top or a balustrade, on which were placed flowerpots containing myrtles, Catalonian jasmine, coxcombs, balsamines, and other odoriferous greenhouse plants. Delicate arbours trailed over the wood to protect it from the heat of the sun. The noble ladies had magnificent terraces attached to their apartments, which were shaded with silk awnings, and alleys formed of orange and lemon trees.

Ghastly and Skulduggery broke off from the group and managed to find a deserted street. Immediately, they boosted themselves up to a terracotta rooftop.

"You cannot kill him," Ghastly said, breaking their silence.

"I cannot kill who?" asked Skulduggery. "Oh, of course. Serpine. Of course I can't. We have our orders, and the Dead Men are known for obeying orders."

"Actually, we're quite notorious for disobeying them."

Skulduggery's head tilted. "We are? I suppose that does sound more like us, if I am to be honest. Yes, you are right. I was thinking of somebody else entirely."

"You understand that we must curtail the urge to disobey for the time being, yes?"

"Absolutely."

"Somehow I don't believe that you do."

"Ghastly, how long have we been friends? A long time, yes? Ever since our encounter with those pirates..." His voice turned wistful. "The open sea, the wind in our faces, the arrogance of youth. We were told what to do back then, do you remember? And we disobeyed, and because of that we plunged into the most excellent of adventures that cast our friendship in iron from that day forth."

"And we almost got a lot of people killed."

"We did, this is true, but that just adds to the frisson, does it not?"

"If we add to the frisson this time round, the results could be too awful to contemplate."

Skulduggery's head tilted in the other direction. "I do not know about that, Ghastly. I can contemplate quite a lot of awfulness."

"If you go after Serpine, I shall have to stop you."

Skulduggery was quiet for a moment before speaking. "So if I attempt to find redress of the man who murdered my family, who then tortured me to death over three long days of indescribable agony, you will physically intervene?"

"To save the rest of the world, I will."

Skulduggery clapped a hand to Ghastly's shoulder. "But of course you will, for you are a decent fellow, and I would expect nothing less." Then he turned and walked to the edge of the building as he took a pouch from his coat.

Ghastly followed him over, watching him sprinkle a handful of rainbow dust into the breeze, then waft it out over the town.

It drifted as a shimmering cloud of ever-changing colour, exactly what one would expect to find in a town this size, where mages mixed with mortals and refrained from public demonstrations of magic. But, as Skulduggery waved his hands and the cloud drifted east, the colour grew stronger, became a deep violet shot through with streams of crimson.

Skulduggery allowed the cloud to dissipate. "I would hazard," he said, "that the Gate to Hell is in that direction."

3

Night fell and lanterns were lit, and the Dead Men and the Masked Sisters followed Skulduggery and Saracen as they guided them deeper into San Gimignano. Skulduggery knew the way and Saracen knew who had swords and knives beneath their coats and cloaks. The closer they got to the *Piazza del Duomo*, the more of Mevolent's sorcerers they had to avoid. By now, the enemy would have realised that one of their companies stationed outside town hadn't reported in, and they'd be on high alert. So far, though, the Dead Men's hard-won experience had allowed them to pass undetected but, should they need a more dramatic way of staying out of sight, Meritorious had gifted them with a cloaking sphere, to use if they found it necessary to get, in Meritorious's own words, "inadvisably close".

They passed into the cathedral, copying the mortals by dropping to their knees and bowing their heads profoundly. In turn, they each seized the holy-water brush and sprinkled and crossed themselves with as much ardour as they could muster. In here, the women tended to wear veils and black gauze hoods, covering their faces but not concealing them, so the Masked Sisters almost fitted right in.

No symphonies played in the cathedral, not like in some of the chapels Ghastly had visited, where the music was so lively it seemed to announce the entry of the ballet or the overture of an opera. The smoke from the lamps obscured the frescoes that told, on one side, the story of the Old Testament and, on the other, the New. The faithful barely looked up as the Dead Men exited the building through another door, before their eyes could start to water. As they reached the next corner, however, Saracen indicated that the time had come.

Shudder took the cloaking sphere from his coat and twisted the hemispheres, and a rippling field of energy expanded outwards, engulfing them all.

Keeping close together, they moved on, coming within touching distance of oblivious sorcerers. Passing through a tunnel and under an arch, they came to a part of town where nature had been allowed to regain control. Beyond a line of trees and ringed by the backs of three narrow-windowed buildings was a large courtyard of green grass and sweet-smelling bushes. Opposite them, across the courtyard, the mouth of a dark tunnel had been cut from the bedrock beneath the north-facing building.

Skulduggery threw a light sprinkling of rainbow dust into the air. The moment it left his gloved fingers, the dust shone with astonishing colours. He pushed the cloud gently, guiding it out through the bubble of invisibility and towards the back of the courtyard. The colours were so vibrant they threatened to hurt Ghastly's eyes.

"*La Porta dell'Inferno,*" Skulduggery muttered.

"I can't see anything," said Dexter.

"It is there," Skulduggery said, moving his hand through the space directly in front of him. "Can you feel it? Right here. A distortion in reality, no bigger than an apple."

"Soldiers are coming," Saracen said. Even though no sound could escape the bubble they were in, he kept his voice to a whisper. "We need to be up higher."

Ghastly, Skulduggery and Ravel used the air to boost them all to the roof of the building on the east side of the courtyard. They crouched there together, watching the tunnel, as Mevolent stepped out of it, into the moonlight.

Every time Ghastly saw him, Mevolent seemed taller than his eight-foot height, and both more slender and more powerful. Today his wig was high parted, white and achingly sophisticated, and he wore a lavishly embroidered waistcoat of such beauty it made Ghastly physically wince with professional jealousy. Mevolent's close-fitting coat reached to his knees, as did the breeches, tailored so finely they didn't seem to even rise up over his stockings with each step. Precious stones decorated the buckles of his shoes, which were square-toed but with a smaller heel than was strictly fashionable. Ghastly liked it, despite himself.

"One well-placed quarrel could end this war," Saracen

muttered, fingers tapping lightly on his crossbow. "The lives we would save. The suffering we would avert."

Ghastly said nothing. It was taking every ounce of his willpower not to jump down and run in. He realised his hands were curled into fists and his jaw was clenched so tight it was painful.

A big man by anyone's reckoning followed Mevolent out, a brute of muscle and scars whose job it was to carry Mevolent's bloody ridiculous sword. The brute stood at over six foot, but the sheathed blade was taller than him, was almost as tall as Mevolent himself. Stupid thing altogether.

Baron Vengeous followed the brute. His coat was buttoned and perfunctory, and in place of a wig he wore a three-cornered hat. One hand rested on the hilt of the cutlass that hung from the sash crossing his broad chest. The first time Ghastly had ever seen a cutlass, it was being swung by a pirate at Ghastly's own head. Since then, he'd failed to develop an affinity for the weapon, quick and manoeuvrable though it was.

After Vengeous came some of his soldiers, and then Nefarian Serpine strolled into the night air. The embroidered elements, patterned like flowers, of his handsome suit matched the waistcoat beneath. He wore his collar high and his sleeves narrow and that red hand of his was gloved, and carried a cane. His wig was long, brushed back off his forehead and tied at the nape of his neck with a black bow.

Ghastly looked over at Skulduggery. Hopeless was beside him, and he seemed ready to spring if Skulduggery did something stupid.

"I'm fine," Skulduggery said. "You do not have to worry about me," and then he lunged and Hopeless dived and brought him down before he made it to the edge of the roof, and Dexter and Saracen piled on and Ghastly hurried over.

"I'm fine," Skulduggery repeated as he struggled out from beneath the jumble. "Absolutely fine." He got one arm free and started to push himself up, but Ghastly seized him by the wrist as Shudder knelt on Skulduggery's head, pinning it to the rooftop. "You do not have to worry about me, gentlemen. Not one bit."

"Skulduggery," said Ravel, kneeling in front of him. "Stop. You've got to stop."

"But I'm not doing anything."

"You are trying to get at Serpine."

"What? How dare you imply such a thing."

"Skulduggery, everyone is on top of you."

"No, they're not. Oh, wait – yes, they are. How odd. I seem to be... ah. I see what has happened. I appear to have slipped. I slipped and fell, and you must have thought I was going to make an attempt on Serpine's life – which is an amusing thought, it is, but so very far from the truth."

"So we can let you up now?"

"Of course you can."

"I mean, if we let you up, do you swear not to attack Serpine?"

Skulduggery was quiet for a few seconds. "Yes," he said eventually.

"Why did you hesitate?"

"I was thinking about it."

"Are you sure you weren't preparing to lie?"

"I wouldn't need to prepare to lie – I would just lie. I am very good at it. But you can trust me – I will not attack Serpine, and I swear I am not lying."

"I don't believe him," said Saracen.

"You realise that you wound me with your words, yes?"

Ghastly took the shackles from his coat and dangled

them in front of Skulduggery's face. "Do we need to chain you? Is that the only way to guarantee you will not disrupt this mission?"

"This mission is a silly mission. It is based on somebody's dreams, for heaven's sake."

"It is based on visions experienced by multiple Sensitives."

"And what is a vision but a waking dream?"

"Skulduggery, I swear..."

"You may let me up," Skulduggery said. "I promise I will not attack Serpine."

There was a moment when each of them considered the risks, and then Ghastly clambered off. One by one, the Dead Men stood, and Ravel pulled Skulduggery to his feet. Shudder checked the cloaking sphere as both hemispheres continued to tick back towards their original positions.

Mevolent and his generals were standing round the spot Skulduggery had identified as the Gate to Hell, and then Mevolent turned and strode back through the tunnel. Vengeous and Serpine issued orders to the soldiers around them, and then they followed their master.

It was at this point that Ghastly realised the Masked Sisters were no longer on the roof.

Frowning, he walked to the other edge of the building, away from the courtyard, and caught a glimpse of running figures. "Damn it," he whispered, and brought the air in to launch himself over to the next rooftop.

He managed a decent landing and ran on, leaping from rooftop to rooftop, plotting a course to intercept the Sisters and whomever they were chasing. When there were no more buildings with rooftops high enough, he dropped to the quiet street and sprinted on.

The man the Sisters were chasing passed in front of him and Ghastly reached out for the spaces between them, but before he could pull the man off his feet Sister Stone caught up to him. She kicked out and the man hit the ground in a whirlwind of limbs. Impressively, he rolled to his feet, but Stone charged into him, and held him while Sister Zeal lashed a kick into the man's midsection. Together they flipped him, snapping a set of shackles on to his wrists. Sister Rapture joined them, breathing heavily through her mask.

"Ah, Mr Bespoke," she said when she noticed Ghastly. "Allow me to introduce you to Mr Abhor."

Stone and Zeal hauled the assassin to his knees.

"Please," said Strickent Abhor, "you're making a huge mistake. You've got to let me kill him. You've got to ̶̶"

Stone hit him, clean across the jaw, and Strickent collapsed.

"And that's enough out of you," she muttered.

4

It was just gone midnight and Strickent Abhor was still unconscious. They'd shackled him to a tree outside town. The whole area was as pretty as a painting, even in the dark, and gave them a beautiful view of San Gimignano sitting on the ridge above them. When it was Ghastly's turn to patrol the perimeter of their camp, Ravel came with him. Ghastly could tell that he had a question – his friend's face was just too honest to disguise it.

"Is there something troubling you, Erskine?"

"Troubling? No," said Ravel. "I would not go so far

as to say that I am troubled. I'm more concerned than anything, but even that concern is barely worth mentioning." They walked on, their way lit by the moon. "However, now that it has actually been mentioned, and now that we are openly discussing it, I admit that I do have a vague *wondering*, one might say. If, by chance, we encounter Serpine, face to face, in our quest to protect Mevolent, do you suppose that Skulduggery will be able to stop himself from killing him on sight?"

"I would like to think so."

"That is not an answer."

"Perhaps not," Ghastly admitted. "What do you think?"

Ravel glanced back at the camp, making sure they were well out of earshot. "I think he will stop himself," he said. "He will want to kill him, obviously. He will want to tear him apart for what he has done. Sometimes I think that it is pure anger that has reanimated Skulduggery's bones. Sometimes I think he is vengeance incarnate. But, no matter his fury, he possesses an intellect of such cold rationality that I believe he will be able to delay the gratification a simple execution would deliver. If what the Grand Mage says is true, if these

Masked Sisters are to be believed, then there are larger forces at play."

Ghastly rubbed his face, feeling the day's worth of bristles. He hated shaving – his scars made it more difficult than it had any right to be – but refused to grow a beard, lest it appear that he was trying, and spectacularly failing, to hide the injuries he'd been born with. "But *are there* wider forces, where Skulduggery is concerned?" he asked. "It has been only thirteen years since Serpine did what he did. I agree with you about the cold rationality part, but I fear not enough time has passed for that side of him to assert itself above the need for retribution."

"If the stakes were not as high, perhaps. But to fail to protect Mevolent would put everyone in the gravest of dangers – us included. I simply do not believe that Skulduggery would do that."

"Have you ever considered," Ghastly said with a smile, "that you hold your friends in too high esteem?"

"Never," said Ravel, giving a smile of his own.

They reached the furthest edge of the perimeter, where it brushed the road. A man on horseback trotted by without seeing them. They split up, taking different routes back to camp. Halfway there, Ghastly passed the

Masked Sisters on their knees, praying to the Lady of Darkness. Sister Stone watched him. He smiled, to assure her that he wasn't going to interrupt. He doubted she smiled back behind her mask.

When he got back to camp, Ravel was already there and Strickent was awake and talking.

"You've got to let me go," he said, his wrists shackled round the other side of the tree at which he sat. "We don't have any time to waste. I have to kill Mevolent."

"And normally we would be all in favour," Ghastly responded, walking up. "Normally, killing Mevolent would be top of our lists of things we would love to do. But a problem has arisen. The women who chased you down, they are the reason we cannot let you do what you want to do, no matter how much we might agree with it. They seem to think that killing Mevolent right now would lead to a catastrophe the likes of which the world has never seen."

"Well," said Skulduggery, his head free of bandages, "it's seen it at least once."

Saracen groaned. "Please, not this again."

Dexter looked genuinely confused. "What are you talking about?"

49

"Skulduggery's giant animal theory. Have you not heard it? A long time ago, according to our learned friend, there were giant animals that walked the Earth."

"Like the Shalgoth?" Dexter asked.

"Not like the Shalgoth," said Skulduggery. "For one thing, the Shalgoth weren't real, and these giant animals were. I have an associate, a Professor of Chemistry at Oxford University, who is in possession of a femur that is, frankly, too large to belong to any known animal."

"And this friend of yours..." said Saracen. "I'm sorry, what's his name again? Richard, is it?"

"Robert."

"Your friend, Robert, this Professor of Chemistry, where does he say this large femur came from?"

Skulduggery's head tilted slightly. "He has a theory that I do not necessarily agree with, but otherwise his judgement is impeccable when it comes to—"

"Where does Robert think the huge leg bone came from, Skulduggery?"

A moment passed. "He thinks the femur came from a giant. Possibly a Titan."

"A Titan," Saracen repeated, failing to stop the delighted grin from spreading across his face. "He thinks the big leg belonged to a god from Greek mythology."

"Or some other type of giant," Skulduggery muttered.

"That does not sound very plausible," Dexter said.

"Ah," Saracen leaped in before Skulduggery could answer, "but that is not what Skulduggery believes. Skulduggery believes that there was a whole race of lizard-animals that ruled the Earth for millions of years, do you not, Skulduggery?"

"The things I have seen have led me to believe these lizards existed, correct," Skulduggery said.

Dexter frowned. "And they ruled the Earth?"

"They were the dominant species, yes."

"So what happened to them?"

"They became extinct. They could have simply died out, absolutely. Or else they might have overfed, used up all their resources. They could have died of disease. But I think it was something else. Something... catastrophic."

"So? How did they die?"

"Vampires."

Dexter's frown deepened. "There were vampires back then?"

"Perhaps," Skulduggery said. "Vampires had to start somewhere, yes? If you ignore the superstitions and the stories about the Witch-Mother cutting off her fingers, we are left with cold, hard science. Millions of years ago, vampires would have been vastly different from the creatures we know today. And maybe it wasn't vampires. It could have been the ancestors of a hundred different monsters. Or it could have been the Ancients themselves, discovering magic and deciding to rid themselves of the giant lizards that kept eating them. I do not know, Dexter. I do not have all the information so I cannot have all the facts, but I am certain that there was an event, there was *something*, that led to the death of every single one of these lizard-animals. A catastrophe, like the one we are apparently facing today."

"You're wrong," said Strickent.

"About what?" Skulduggery asked. "The lizard-animals? You actually think it was the leg of a Titan?"

Strickent shook his head. "I'm not the one who's going to be responsible for the catastrophe. I have... I'm no Sensitive, but I worship the Hidden God, praise him and his name. He allowed me to see, in a vision, Mevolent widening the Gate to Hell. I have seen what emerges. I have seen *who* emerges."

Ghastly raised an eyebrow. "The Masked Sisters have Sensitives of their own, Strickent. They tell the same story, that Mevolent opens wide *La Porta dell'Inferno,* but their story continues with you killing Mevolent before he can correct his mistake and seal it again. Disaster follows."

Strickent laughed. "So you've been commanded to stop me from stopping Mevolent? The Masked Sisters worship the Lady of Darkness. That's who is trapped behind the Gate to Hell. That's who will emerge. Do you understand? *You cannot trust them.* I'm here to stop Mevolent before he can open the Gate wide enough so that she can step into our reality, which is exactly what's going to happen if you do not let me go. I've seen how I kill Mevolent, and I've seen when I do it. It is not this night, so it's not too late to save us all."

Ghastly hesitated, and looked at his brothers-in-arms.

"Our Council of Elders agree with the Masked Sisters," said Shudder.

"Then the Sisters have duped them," said Strickent.

"Our own Sensitives have confirmed what they say."

Strickent shook his head. "I don't... I don't know how that can be."

"Sensitives are trained to decipher their dreams and interpret their visions," Skulduggery said. "Sometimes things are not what they appear to be. Maybe you did not fully understand the vision you had."

"I understood it well enough."

"But you are not trained, are you?"

"As a Sensitive? No, I'm not."

"Then you may be mistaken."

"Is it possible that I'm mistaken? Yes, I'll accept that. But I know in my heart, I know in my soul, that what the Hidden God has shown me will come to pass unless I stop Mevolent."

"We could ask the Sisters," said Hopeless.

Ghastly looked at him. "You believe what he says?"

Hopeless shrugged. "He seems sincere. Sincerely confused, at any rate. Maybe we should talk to the Sisters, ask them to respond to his accusations, and see what they say. If we believe them, then we obey the orders we have been given. If we do not..."

Ghastly grunted. "If we do not, we get to assassinate Mevolent. I like this plan."

5

The Sisters were just finishing their prayers when Ghastly walked up.

"Sister Rapture," he said, "could I have a word?"

"Of course." She glanced at the other two. "I will meet you back at camp."

They nodded and moved off, and Sister Rapture indicated ahead of them. "Would you like to go for a walk, Mr Bespoke?"

"I would love to," he said. "And you can call me Ghastly, if it pleases you."

"I would like that," she said.

They started walking. Laughter and voices drifted to them from the town walls. Above them, a bat circled.

"Our guest," said Ghastly, "Mr Abhor. He is saying some interesting things."

"He is?"

"He is levelling some accusations."

"Ah." The moonlight caught her eyes behind the mask, and made them sparkle. "He's telling you horrible stories about the Masked Sisters, is he? He says, perhaps, that you cannot trust us? He is asking how you can trust those whose faces you cannot see?"

"Faces are overrated," said Ghastly. "The one I possess is ruined beyond measure, and my very good friend doesn't have one at all."

"I would not say yours is ruined, Ghastly. I would not say that at all."

Ghastly smiled. "I confess, I know little about your religion, and even less about your sect."

Rapture raised her hands to the night sky. "We pray to the Lady of Darkness, she who has birthed the world and the moon, and the stars that surround them. She is the darkness between all things, the shadow that protects us from the harsh light, the shade that cools us from the oppressive heat. She is the night, and she loves us very much."

"And what does she want in return?"

"She wants nothing."

"All gods want something," Ghastly said. "Adoration. Worship. Souls."

"The Lady of Darkness wants none of these things."

"And what of your sect? What do you want?"

"Simply to love the Lady in return."

"And to spread the word of your religion?"

She watched him. "You think we have unpleasant motives, Ghastly. You think we are after power or influence purely because that is what you are used to. You have seen religions and churches and sects like ours accumulating wealth and property for those who wear the vestments, who call themselves priests or priestesses or popes or archdeacons..."

"And you are saying that none of this interests you?"

"That is exactly what we're saying."

"And why do you wear the masks?"

"To disappear," Rapture replied. "My sisters and I, we prefer to be subsumed by our love, so we surrender our faces for years at a time, leaving our vanities to one side and giving the Lady our uncompromised devotion. This is not something we expect from others, by the way, and, despite being known as the Masked Sisters, not all of us wear these masks. It is a personal choice."

"Strickent told us that the Lady of Darkness waits beyond the Gate to Hell."

Behind those eyeholes in the mask, a frown. "I see. And he saw this in a vision?"

"So he says."

"And what did he say happens?"

"He says Mevolent opens the gate and the Lady of Darkness emerges. He says you are trying to prevent him from stopping her. If this were true, Rapture, what would the Lady of Darkness want once released?"

"Nothing, as far as I am aware. But you must understand, Ghastly, the Lady of Darkness is not a person. She is not one being. She is, instead, everything. She is all around us at every moment. She would not need to take human form because... well, she does not have to."

"Then why would Strickent say this?"

"I genuinely do not know. Maybe the vision confused him."

Ghastly nodded. "That was Skulduggery's suggestion. Strickent worships the Hidden God – do you know anything about that?"

"I have never heard of such a god," she replied, "and I have heard of a lot of gods and met many people who worship them. Throw a pebble in any fair-sized city and you are likely to hit a worshipper of the Faceless Ones or the Christ or Allah – but the lesser-known gods, the smaller religions, they have their zealots, too. When I was a child, I knew a boy whose family idolised the Deathless, a farmer who worshipped Gog Magog and a woman who prayed to the Arok-Nar. But the Hidden God? I'm afraid he must be living up to his name.

"Besides, it's not just *our* Sensitives who foresaw the consequences of Mevolent's assassination. Your own psychics agree."

"But our own psychics only saw what's going to happen once you had arrived with your warnings," said Ghastly.

"Do you think we interfered in some way?"

"It is possible."

"So you no longer trust us?"

"I am merely keeping an open mind."

"Doubting us is one thing," Rapture said. "Scepticism is a generally healthy trait to have. But, if this doubt leads to any harm befalling Mevolent before he has a chance to seal *La Porta dell'Inferno*, I'm afraid that is where trouble lies."

"We are not planning on harming Mevolent, and we are not planning on letting Strickent harm Mevolent," Ghastly assured her. "There's a Sensitive in town that we can pay to send word to Meritorious regarding our concerns, and we are going to be keeping a close eye on what is going on, but until we hear differently we will obey orders."

Rapture took a deep breath, and exhaled. "That is... acceptable, I suppose. So long as you can guarantee that you will not interfere with Mevolent."

"Providing we see no reason to, we shall remain at a distance. You have my word."

They made their way back to camp and Ghastly's face started to hurt, and as they sat on the ground and talked softly he realised why: he was smiling, and he was so very unused to smiling.

They went to sleep, the Dead Men and the Masked Sisters, with Skulduggery standing watch as he always did, and Ghastly dreamed good dreams and woke early, just after dawn. He couldn't see Skulduggery and that was fine. When he got to his feet and realised that Strickent Abhor was no longer shackled to the tree, however, all the good feelings fled from his heart.

He turned, and glared at the walled town on the hill.

6

"I hope this wasn't planned," said Rapture as they readied the horses. She kept her voice low so that Sister Zeal and Sister Stone didn't hear.

"I swear to you, Skulduggery acted of his own accord," said Ghastly. "He has a personal grudge against Serpine that has obviously clouded his judgement."

Rapture nodded. "His own murder, and the murder of his wife and child. I am aware of the history."

"We should have been more careful. I apologise."

Dexter was first into the saddle, but then Hopeless came forward, stopping him from riding off.

"What are you doing?" Dexter asked. "We have no time to delay."

"Skulduggery and Strickent are hours ahead of us," Hopeless said. "We can afford another few minutes to discuss our plans."

"You have something to propose?" asked Ravel, leading his horse closer.

"We have a choice to make," Hopeless said. "Our first option is to let Skulduggery and Strickent assassinate Mevolent – and presumably Serpine, too, while they are at it."

"That is unacceptable," said Sister Zeal.

Hopeless nodded. "I imagined so. Or we can try to quietly hunt them down, though this is Skulduggery Pleasant we're talking about, so I do not like our chances of stopping them in time. Our third option is to get a warning to Mevolent about the threat to his life, making it serious enough for him to increase security, but not so serious as to cause him to leave town before sealing the Gate to Hell. Three options. Raise your hands for option one."

Dexter was the only one to put up his hand.

"And now for option two?"

Saracen, Ravel and Dexter all raised their hands.

Shudder frowned up at Dexter. "You can't vote twice."

"But I was the only one to vote for the first option, so I would like to take it back and use it now, because option two actually has a chance of winning."

Shudder shook his head. "You have already voted, and you wasted it. You cannot use it again."

"Then just pretend I haven't voted yet."

"We cannot pretend."

"Of course you can."

"That is not how this works."

"Anton," Hopeless said, "you know how this will end."

Shudder sighed. "Fine. Dexter casts his vote for option two."

"Thank you," Dexter said with a smile. "Remind me what option two was?"

"We try to find Skulduggery and Strickent before they kill Mevolent," said Hopeless. "And option three is to warn Mevolent somehow, which gets my vote. Anyone else?"

Ghastly and Shudder put up their hands, and so did Dexter.

"You can't vote for everything," Shudder said immediately.

"But the third option is the most sensible."

"You already voted for the second option," said Saracen.

"Because both have their merits."

"I vote for option three," said Rapture. "As do Zeal and Stone."

Ravel frowned. "I do not think you get a vote, though. Do they get a vote? I do not think they should. And, if they do, it should only count as one, since I would imagine they would vote the same way no matter what."

"Not necessarily," said Rapture.

"Have we decided if Dexter is allowed to vote for option three?" asked Saracen.

"Dexter cannot vote for a third time," Ghastly said, "and the Masked Sisters only get one vote – which leaves us with three votes for option two, and four votes for option three. So we find a way to get Mevolent to increase his security. Does anyone have any ideas as to how to do this?"

The Sisters talked quietly among themselves, and finally Rapture nodded to Ghastly. "We ask Meritorious to bring his army up to the town's borders. They do not set foot inside – we don't want fighting to break out – but every last one of Mevolent's soldiers will be on high alert, including his personal guard. Skulduggery and Strickent will be prevented from getting close, so Mevolent should be able to continue his examination of the Gate to Hell without interruption."

When no objections were raised, Ghastly nodded. "Very well. We shall locate the Sensitive and have him send our message to Meritorious. Saracen, Dexter, I'll need you with me."

"I will accompany you," said Rapture. "If you have no objections?"

Ghastly smiled. "By all means."

They rode to the main gate on the south-facing ridge, left the horses there and walked in. While Ghastly dodged the carts and drays that crowded the street and tried deciphering the directions on the thick, folded paper he'd been carrying in his pocket for days, Saracen smiled at Sister Rapture.

"I have always found people of faith to be extremely attractive," he said. "Even the masked ones."

"Oh," she replied.

"I think it's something about their sheer capacity for love. They are brimming with it – overflowing with so much compassion that they are capable of redirecting it to a force beyond their senses, to a being or a pantheon of beings they cannot prove even exists, and yet they love them anyway."

"That is what faith means."

"Exactly!" Saracen said, laughing. The laugh turned to a smoulder. "*Exactly*."

"I have a question," said Dexter. "Your Lady of Darkness – where did she come from?"

"She has always been here," Rapture replied, "and the universe grew in her shadow."

"So she was here before the universe came into being? Before existence? Does your faith explain how it's possible for someone to exist before existence was created? Who created her? How long had she been standing around before she decided to make a universe?"

"Those are really good questions, Mr Vex."

"Do you have any answers for me?"

"We have a few books about it, yes," Rapture said, "but, in order to understand, you must first reorder your thinking. Before the Lady of Darkness, there was nothing. No planets, no stars, no cosmos. There was not even the space between them – for emptiness is still a thing, and there were no things. The universe, when she created it, brought with it this idea we call time. The cosmic clock only started ticking once there was a universe to age. So there were no endless eons that passed before reality came to be – because there was no time. There was simply the Lady of Darkness."

Dexter said nothing for a while, then nudged Saracen. "Back to you."

"Now, tell me this and tell me no more," Saracen said. "Is the Masked Sisters a celibate order, or is it one of the fun ones I've been hearing about?"

"I have another question," Ghastly interrupted hastily. "What do we think Skulduggery will do if he meets Serpine before our mission is complete?"

"Kill him," said Saracen.

"Prioritise the mission," said Dexter.

"We have a wager, actually," Saracen said. "Would

you care to be a part of it? I firmly believe that Skulduggery will be unable to stop himself from exacting his violent and blood-soaked revenge."

Dexter shook his head. "Whereas I believe he will be able to put the good of the mission ahead of his own needs. I think he has proven himself to us by now."

"The only thing Skulduggery has proven himself to be is multifaceted," Saracen countered. "The same can be said for any of us. We are steadfast to a point, and beyond that point we are completely unpredictable. Am I certain that Skulduggery would kill Serpine, despite what it would mean to our mission? No, I am not. But am I comfortable with my assertion that the inherent unpredictability that drives all of us, and Skulduggery is no exception, could result in this aforementioned violent and blood-soaked revenge? I am, indeed."

"You," said Dexter, "are a cynic."

"This is true," Saracen agreed. "But so is Skulduggery, and as such I feel I may have the advantage in anticipating his actions. Remember, Dexter – I know things."

"If you truly knew things, then you would never lose a wager, and you lose our wagers all the time."

"I know some of the things," Saracen said, shrugging. "Not all of the things."

"I told you," said a man from behind them.

They turned to see four men and three women taking down their hoods. Their faces were weather-beaten and nicked with old cuts. Their noses were bent and some of their teeth were missing. These were people who knew battle.

"Once you've seen those scars," said the man in front, "you don't forget them. That's Ghastly Bespoke, that is. The handsome one's Dexter Vex. The other's Saracen Rue."

"Hey," said Saracen.

"Don't know who the filly in the mask is," the man continued, "but if she's covering up beside Ghastly Bespoke she must be ugly indeed!"

The group laughed, putting a little too much enthusiasm into it for it to be genuine.

"I'm sorry," said Ghastly, "you have us at a disadvantage."

"You're right," said one of the women. "We do. There's a hundred of us here in this bloody town, and there's only four of you. That's definitely a disadvantage, if you ask me."

Ghastly smiled. "We are simply passing through. We do not know you, and we do not know what you are about. We are on our way to meet a friend, and then we are travelling onwards, to Pisa."

The man spoke again. "We're soldiers."

"An honourable profession, no doubt. And a lucrative one, I should imagine! There is always a war on somewhere in the world, am I right?"

"We don't fight in mortal wars," the woman sneered. "We fight in our war."

"Again, my friends, we do not know you, and we do not—"

"We fight for Mevolent."

Ghastly sagged and the soldiers laughed.

"Can't talk your way out of this now, can you?" said the woman. "Can't walk away, eh?"

"No," said Ghastly. "Now we have to fight."

"Not so fast," said the man, holding up a hand. "Why should we all fall upon each other, blade to blade, fist to fist, hacking and cutting and gouging and tearing? Are we barbarians? Are we animals?"

"You have an alternative?"

"Indeed I do. Our champion against yours."

"And what do the winners get?"

"The chance to walk out of here without further bloodshed."

"And the losers?"

"They surrender their weapons and become our prisoners."

Ghastly thought about it. "And this contest – it takes place out of the sight of mortals?"

The man grinned. "It just so happens there's a quiet street behind this one. We block off both ends: no one will see who's not supposed to."

"And the contest... it is to the death, I presume?"

"To the death, yes. One condition: we each pick the other's champion."

"Dead Men only," said Ghastly. Rapture went to say something, but Ghastly cut her off. "I mean you no disrespect, but I have never seen you fight, so I cannot vouch for you."

"Dead Men only," said the man. "Absolutely."

Ghastly looked to Saracen and Dexter, and they nodded. Rapture merely glowered.

"We have a deal," said Ghastly.

Keeping a wary eye on each other, they all moved one street over, away from the mortals.

"Name your warriors," said the grinning man.

"You know our names," Ghastly answered. "Ghastly, Dexter and Saracen."

The soldiers glanced at one another, whispered, and the man's grin grew wider. "We choose Saracen as your champion."

"Bugger!" Saracen exclaimed.

"And our warriors," said the man. "Délicat, Adeline, Heartchopper, Heinous, Turlough, Trocious and Snake."

Ghastly turned to the others and spoke softly. "I assume, Saracen, that you would rather avoid fighting to the death with a woman."

"What?" he responded. "Why? No disrespect, Sister Rapture, but all those men are large and scary, and the women are small and, by the looks of things, physically weaker. I would probably do better against them were this to devolve into a matter of physical strength. Certainly, I would stand a better chance of not dying."

"Saracen," said Dexter, "you cannot choose to fight a woman to the death."

"Why not?"

"It's... Because it is... Ghastly, explain to him."

"It is not chivalrous," said Ghastly.

Saracen blinked. "If I fight a woman on the battlefield, do you not expect me to kill her?"

"That... that is what we expect, yes."

"And would you not, in a life-or-death struggle with a female, kill her to prevent her from killing you?"

Dexter sighed. "Absolutely, we would."

"Then what, may I ask, is so bad about actually choosing to fight a woman in a duel?"

"Because it is not..."

"Not what?"

"It is not *nice*."

"It is a duel!" Saracen said. "To the death! There is *nothing* about this that is nice!"

"I agree with him," said Rapture.

Ghastly waited for Saracen to change his mind. When he didn't, he shook his head. "Very well. Fight a woman, then. Do you have a preference for which one?"

"What were their names?" Saracen asked.

"Délicat, Adeline and... something."

"Heinous," said Dexter. "Or maybe Heartchopper's the third one."

They took a quick glance at the soldiers.

"I think Délicat is the small one with the blonde hair," said Rapture, "and Adeline is the one with the unsmiling face."

"Which means Heartchopper or Heinous is the one in front," said Dexter. "I would advise you not to fight that one, Saracen."

Saracen nodded. "I agree. She's scary. As is the unsmiling one. Very well, I have made my decision." He stepped forward. "We choose Délicat as your champion," he announced loudly.

The huge man at the back with all the muscles clapped his ridiculously massive hands with delight.

"Bugger!" Saracen exclaimed again.

7

"I am Délicat Verdure," the huge soldier said in French as he walked forward. "I am the last of my line, a killer of killers, descended from the Faceless Ones themselves when they walked the Earth in flesh and blood. I am here to fight for my Lord Mevolent, to ensure the return of my people to power. I am here to dig my hand into your chest and pull out your heart. I am here to pulverise your skull and scoop out the brain it carries, and then stand on that brain, to churn it beneath my heel. These are all the things I will do to you. It is not a warning;

it is not a threat. It is merely a list. Now we fight, and you die." Délicat drew his sword.

"I am Saracen Rue," Saracen said, also in French. He remembered to step forward as he continued. "I am descended from my parents. I cannot remember the list of things you have just said because I was too busy being intimidated by all the muscles you have, so I do not have much of a retort. The only thing I will say is that you probably spell your name without an *e* at the end of it, would I be correct? It's just, it would have been nice to know your name was the masculine form of the word, that's all. It would have been advantageous to have seen it written down. But what is done is done. Such is life." Saracen drew his sword.

The grinning man and his soldiers backed up to seal off one end of the street. Ghastly, Dexter and Rapture did the same with the other.

Saracen met Délicat in the middle.

"Before we begin," Saracen said, "a quick word about the rules..."

Délicat roared and lunged and swung and Saracen yelped and skipped out of the way, and Ghastly watched him manoeuvre, deflecting when he had to as Délicat advanced, his face contorted with hatred. Saracen, for his part, merely looked startled, but Ghastly didn't mind that. Saracen had a tendency to look startled whenever he fought, like he was astonished that anyone would want to hurt him.

Saracen twisted and stumbled and they broke apart.

"You fight like an old man," said Délicat.

"An old man who is really good at fighting?" Saracen asked, a little too hopefully.

"No."

Beating back the disappointment on his face was at least a fight Saracen stood a chance of winning – this Délicat was far too big and far too strong and far too quick for Saracen to handle without cheating. Now Ghastly was worried. Dexter didn't seem overly concerned, however.

"Use your magic on him," he called. "Go on. See how far 'knowing things' will get you against a barbarian with a sword."

"You are not helping," Saracen said, dodging a swipe.

"Your friend would appear to be outclassed," Rapture said quietly.

Ghastly nodded. "Saracen is a rare breed of warrior.

Pit him against two opponents, three, four – he will beat them handily. Pit him against only one and, historically, he struggles."

"That's quite a drawback for a soldier."

"It definitely can be," Ghastly said as Délicat's sword sliced through Saracen's coat. "He needs the danger to be amplified, you see. Unless he knows that he is about to die, he finds it difficult to rise to the occasion."

"And yet, if his life is most at risk when fighting only one opponent," Rapture responded, "one would imagine that this would provide all the danger he requires."

"One would imagine," Ghastly said, shrugging.

Saracen tried dancing away from Délicat's next attack, tripped over his own feet and tumbled, before jumping back up. "I meant to do that," he announced.

"Stop moving," said Délicat, "and I will make this quick."

Saracen laughed. "You fool. You fool! I am but toying with you. You are my idiotic plaything, lumbering around this makeshift arena of ours, falling into my every trap."

Délicat stalked him. "And yet you are the one with blood leaking from gashes I have gifted you."

"Mere scratches," said Saracen, grinning. "I give myself worse every morning when I shave my bristles."

"He does," Dexter said from the sidelines. "He's not very good at shaving."

"I engaged you in combat so as to loosen my limbs and stretch my muscles," Saracen said, "but you provide little in the way of a challenge. Maybe your friends can help? What say you, noble warriors? Would some of you care to join your companion in his attempts to inflict harm upon my person?"

"I don't need them to kill you," Délicat snarled.

"Believe me, sir," Saracen replied, "you most assuredly do."

Délicat gave a single shake of his head. "Very well. If you wish to die all the sooner, we will combine our efforts. I grow tired of chasing you."

Saracen's grin widened. "Splendid."

"Snake," said Délicat, "Trocious, Heartchopper – please come and join the merriment."

Snake, the grinning man, pulled his sword. Trocious, a gentleman with a beard as fierce as his axe, followed him into the fight. The unsmiling woman kissed her blade before joining them.

Ghastly raised an eyebrow at Rapture. "This has always been Saracen's particular skill," he told her.

"Goading people into unnecessary violence?"

"Precisely."

Saracen waited until Délicat and his friends had him completely surrounded, and then he tossed his sword to one side and stood with his arms wide. Délicat rolled his eyes a little, and stepped in with an overhead swing.

Saracen turned, letting the swing pass him. He gripped Délicat's arm and dodged the axe that came for his back, ramming his elbow into the hinge of Délicat's jaw as he did so. Almost too quickly to discern, he ran his free hand down the length of the bigger man's arm, and all of a sudden he was holding Délicat's sword. Steel clashed with steel as he defended, one-handed, the stilted, awkward jabs of the other three, swinging Délicat around like a rag-doll shield, despite his size. Trocious cursed as another clean swing of his axe was foiled by his friend getting in the way, and the curse turned to a gurgle when the tip of Saracen's purloined sword sank into his chest.

Trocious collapsed and Saracen threw Délicat on top of him, allowing Snake and Heartchopper their first straight line of attack. They leaped in and Saracen disarmed Snake and tripped Heartchopper. Snake released a stream of energy from his hand, and Saracen took that hand off as he spun, burying his sword in the neck of Heartchopper. He left his sword where it was, grabbed her sword as it fell, and rammed it through Snake's torso, who was probably thankful that now he had something to take his mind off his missing hand.

Délicat roared and dived at Saracen with a knife in his fist and Saracen hit him, head-butted him and threw him, pressing Délicat's own knife deep into his neck.

Then he stood, eyes on the dying soldier, who made one last sound before going quiet.

The others – Adeline, Heinous and Turlough – took out their weapons and roared as they came running. Dexter let loose with an energy stream that caught one of the women – either Adeline or Heinous – straight in the face, flipping her over. Saracen deflected Turlough's attack and sent him stumbling towards Sister Rapture, who slid a knife into his chest. The remaining woman – either Heinous or Adeline – had second thoughts about the whole thing and turned to run. Ghastly waved his hand and a gust of wind smacked her into the wall.

As she lay in a crumpled heap, trying to get the air back into her lungs, Ghastly crouched by her. "Are you Heinous?" he asked.

"Adeline," she gasped.

"Adeline, you have a choice. You could either be shackled and taken prisoner and spend the remainder of the war growing old in a cell, or you could tell us where to find someone we're looking for. I have directions, but they are not very clear. He's a Sensitive, this person, and lives somewhere—"

"I know him," Adeline managed. "I can take you."

"That is very nice of you."

"She will lead us into a trap," said Rapture.

"I won't," Adeline responded, shaking her head. "I swear."

Ghastly frowned. "I would like to believe you, but Sister Rapture does have a point."

"He's an old man, the Sensitive. Old and grumpy. I know him. I've spoken to him."

"You know him but you haven't killed him?" Dexter asked.

She glared. "We don't just kill people. Why would we kill him? He's a mage, like us."

"He could be a threat."

"If he became one," said Adeline, "we would kill him then. But why would we kill someone who was not a threat to us?"

"You kill mortals all the time."

"Because they are a threat. Because, if they knew about us, they would hang us and burn us." She was breathing easier now, and sat up straighter. "I know what you think. You think you're all good and noble while we are all evil. You think Mevolent is the devil – but Mevolent is our saviour. He will deliver us to a paradise of our own making."

"At the expense of everyone else."

"I'm sorry, do you expect me to debate this with you while all my friends are lying dead around me?"

"You and your friends started it," Saracen reminded her.

"I'm not denying that. All I am saying is that it's difficult to formulate a cogent argument immediately after watching some of my best friends get killed."

"I was acting in self-defence."

"Again, I am not denying that. I fully realise that we forced this upon you. I acknowledge that we wanted to kill some of you and deliver the rest of you to Mevolent.

But it doesn't change the fact that I grew up with Délicat and Trocious. They were like my brothers. And now... now they're..." She stopped, tears in her eyes.

Saracen looked at Ghastly. "I admit, I am not sure what is expected of me in this moment."

Ghastly picked Adeline off the ground and shackled her hands behind her back. "Miss, I understand that the enormity of what has happened is now settling upon you. I understand that you are currently going through an awful lot. My sympathy is not what it would be for an innocent victim of violence, but it is not non-existent, either. That said, you have one chance to avoid a prison cell, and that is to take us to the Sensitive."

"And then you'll let me go?"

"We will give you a horse and escort you as far as we can and allow you to ride on. But if you return, Adeline, if we see you in town again, if you come back to warn Mevolent that we are here..."

"I know," said Adeline. "You don't have to say it."

"Oh, but I do," Ghastly responded. "Adeline, we will kill you like we killed your friends. Do you believe me?"

She looked into his eyes, and nodded.

"Good," he said. "Lead the way."

8

Adeline took them to a small house on the edge of town, close to the north-west wall. An old donkey stood outside, tied to a post. It appeared disinterested in their business. Ghastly knocked on the open door. An old man sat sleeping inside, in the draught that travelled from the front door to the window behind.

"Hello?" Ghastly said. "Hello?" he said again, louder.

The old man slept with his head thrown back. He made unsettling noises with his throat.

Ghastly led the way in. Everyone stepped quietly, so

as not to wake him. They put Adeline on the floor in the corner and tied her ankles so she couldn't run. On the table was an empty cup and a plate of dates. A fly buzzed from one to the other, enjoying itself immensely.

"Excuse me?" said Dexter. The old man stayed asleep. Dexter looked at the others. "What should we do?"

"Poke him with something," said Saracen.

Ghastly frowned. "Why would we poke the man when we can just wake him by talking louder?" He turned back to the Sensitive and cleared his throat, and Saracen picked up a date from the table and lobbed it without aiming and it dropped into the old man's open mouth.

Immediately, the Sensitive sat bolt upright, spluttering, then leaned over and hacked and coughed towards the floor. Ghastly glared at Saracen, who at least had the decency to look extremely sorry.

Gasping now, his throat cleared, the old man collapsed back into his chair and regarded them with watery-eyed suspicion.

"Hello," Ghastly said again, smiling this time. "Are you Rima Stranza?"

"That is what they call me, when they bother to call

me anything," said the old man. "When they need something from me."

"You're a Sensitive?"

"I am, yes. Who are you and what are you doing in my hovel?"

"You can see the future," Dexter answered. "Do you not know who we are?"

"I'm a Sensitive," said Rima, "but I don't work for free. If I'm going to peer into either the future or people's minds, I'm going to get paid for it. Do you know how much it hurts, peering into a mind? Do you have any idea about the headaches it causes? Sometimes I have to lie down in a dark room for days. Days!"

"That sounds awful," said Rapture.

"It feels like there's a bird in my head screaming to be let out."

"Well, we are happy to pay. My name is Rapture. This is Ghastly, Dexter and Saracen."

"And who is that in the corner?"

"She is our prisoner. She will not be speaking."

"Prisoner, eh? I see. So have you got something to do with all these violent thoughts I've been catching glimpses of lately?"

"What violent thoughts are those?"

"I see a tall, tall man with hair the colour of pale gold, and this man is filled with death."

"That's Mevolent," said Ghastly.

Rima stuck a finger in his ear and wiggled it about. "Is he bad?"

"You haven't heard of Mevolent?"

"There are hundreds of people in the world. I don't feel the need to know them all."

"Um... there are more than hundreds of people in the world."

Rima frowned, finger still in his ear. "How many more?"

"Probably, I don't know, five or six hundred million."

"Million? What's a million? Is that more than a hundred?"

"Significantly."

"And you say there are five or six hundred of these millions of people in the world? Are you sure? Have you met all of them?"

"Well, no..."

"Then how do you know there aren't just a few hundred? My family used to have sheep, and, when you'd try to count the sheep, sometimes you'd count the same one twice because they kept moving around. This was after we'd learned to count, of course. Before that, we'd just stand in the field, looking at them. We knew there was a difference between *lots of sheep* and *not very many sheep at all*, and that's how we kept track. I'm telling you, learning to count solved so many problems for my family. There were eight of us in all, but my parents didn't know that until I was fourteen. I think I was fourteen anyway. We'd only learned to count the previous summer, so much of it was guesswork." Rima removed his finger from his ear and examined it.

"Mevolent is the one we are fighting against," Ghastly said when he was sure the Sensitive had finished talking.

"And why are you fighting against him?"

Dexter frowned. "You are aware that there's a war on, are you not?"

"There is? Where?"

"All around us."

Rima gave his finger a tentative lick, then wiped it on his trousers. "I can't say I've noticed."

"It has been going on for one hundred and twelve years."

"And is it nearly over?"

"It's a war. We will not know when it's over until it's over."

"What's it about, then, this war?"

"Mevolent wants to bring the Faceless Ones back and enslave the mortals, and the rest of us are fighting to stop that from happening."

"This Mevolent fellow believes in the Faceless Ones?"

"He does, and so do a lot of his followers."

Rima sniffed, unimpressed. "They're not very clever, then, are they, if they believe in children's stories? When I was a child, we believed that there was this unseen force that draws objects towards the centre of the Earth, but we grew out of that, didn't we?"

"Uh," said Ghastly, "there *is* an unseen force that draws objects towards the centre of the Earth."

"I'm sorry? There's what?"

"An Indian mathematician—"

"Brahmagupta," said Saracen.

"—yes, thank you, Brahmagupta, he proposed the idea over a thousand years ago. Actually, only very recently, Isaac Newton took that idea and carried it forward. He published the *Mathematical Principles of Natural Philosophy*, where he—"

"Haven't read it," said Rima.

"No, well, in it he explains how this universal force, which he calls gravity, means that the planets are kept—"

"Is it written in Latin?" asked Rima.

"Uh, yes."

"I don't read Latin. It's a dying language, you mark my words."

"I think it is also available in Italian, maybe? I am not sure. I read it in its original Latin."

"Of course you did," Rima said, rolling his eyes.

"We were wondering if you could help us," Rapture interrupted. "We want to get a message to the Sanctuary in Ireland."

"You are aware of such things called boats, aren't you? Send your message on one of those."

"We need the message delivered today."

"You're asking me to send a psychic message to a country I've never been, to someone I've never met? Do you know the headache that will cause?"

"We will pay you."

"It's not about the money."

"Then what is it about?"

"It's about what the money can buy."

"Then what do you want us to buy you?"

Rima peered at them through narrowed eyes. "This house, it's old. It is old and crumbling and when I sit here in my chair in the winter it's too cold and I am uncomfortable, and when I sit here in the summer it's too hot and, again, I am uncomfortable. It's an awful house and I hate it."

Ghastly frowned. "You want us to buy you a house?"

"Don't be ridiculous," said Rima. "If I charged people a house every time they wanted me to do something, I would either have many houses or none at all. No. Beside my house, you may have passed it on your way in, is a post. Tied to that post is a donkey. The donkey is tired and grumpy and far too bony, so that when I come in after a long journey my backside is sore and it makes sitting in my chair even more uncomfortable than it usually is."

"Then you want us to buy you a donkey?" asked Ghastly.

"Why would I need a donkey? I have one outside, tied to a post. If I had two, I'd need another post, and one post is enough for a man like me. Please pay attention. Upon the donkey is a blanket. The blanket is ragged and smelly and is home to many moths. It offers scant protection from the bony horse which, again, makes sitting in my chair uncomfortable."

Ghastly waited, then said, "Do you want us to buy you a blanket?"

"I can buy my own blankets, thank you very much," said Rima.

"Then what do you want?"

"If you'll let me finish, perhaps I can get to that!" Rima breathed out, and continued. "I bought the blanket from a stall in the market twenty years ago. The woman who sold it to me is dead now – she died by falling off a cart, into a ditch. The ditch is unimportant. The cart belonged to a man with two legs. I mention the legs because the legs are important. The man has a twin, identical in every way, except this twin has only one leg, having lost the other one by falling off a different cart, some years earlier. The twin lives across from me, over there." Rima pointed out through the open door, at the house on the other side of the street. "He is selling a chair. I would very much like to own this chair because, as I have repeatedly hinted at and yet you have somehow failed to notice, the chair I'm sitting in now is very uncomfortable. That is the price you must pay."

Ghastly blinked. "We shall buy you the chair."

Rima folded his arms. "I've been fooled before, by people promising to buy me a chair after I've done what they needed me to do. Then, once I've delivered upon my promise, they walk away, shouting back at me that I'm a Sensitive, and why didn't I see that coming? To which my answer is always the same: I do not use my power without getting paid for it." His shoulders sagged. "But they're always out of earshot by that stage."

"I shall go and buy the chair," said Dexter, and he went across the street.

"We'll wait here, then," said Rima, glaring at them suspiciously.

Saracen tried smiling. "Nice day, is it not?"

"It's too hot," said Rima.

"There are some clouds moving in from the east, so it might rain later."

"If you want me to confirm that, you'll need to buy me another chair."

Saracen went quiet, and Dexter came back.

"Here you go," he said, putting the chair down. Rima gazed at it for a bit, then got up, moved over, and sat down. He spent close to a minute squirming his buttocks into it, then finally relaxed back.

Rapture smiled. "Is that better?"

"No," he said. "It's even more uncomfortable than the other one. I suppose I should have sat in it before I got you to buy it, but a deal's a deal. What message do you wish to send?"

9

Shielding one's thoughts from a Sensitive's casual scan was difficult, but not impossible. This meant that a small group of mages could sneak by such a Sensitive, so long as the Sensitive was not actively searching for them.

Shielding an army from a Sensitive, however, fell into the category of 'practically impossible' – meaning that it could be done in theory, but it had never actually been managed. There was always some soldier, in the middle of it all, who lost focus at a critical moment, or got distracted, or just wasn't very good at remaining hidden when the pressure was on. The Sensitive would detect him, probe further, and suddenly every last one of the soldiers would light up like they were holding flaming torches in an open field at night.

When Meritorious and his army teleported to the hills south of San Gimignano, hidden from view with cloaking spheres, Mevolent's Sensitives detected them immediately. Soldiers in civilian clothes rushed to the town walls, swords and axes and cudgels held inside coats while the mortals carried on around them, oblivious to the rising hostility. Baron Vengeous strode to one of the gates, stood with his legs apart, daring the enemy to come at him. The threat was clear. Cross this boundary, loose even one arrow or throw even one ball of fire, and the people of this town would be the first to die.

Meritorious and his army stayed invisible and kept back. Mevolent's soldiers secured the perimeter all the way round the town and prepared to repel an assault. The Dead Men and the Masked Sisters had a bad supper of liver and brains, though as to what animals they belonged, none of them could guess. Once their unsatisfactory meal was over, they found an abandoned house in which to wait for the alarm to die down. Ravel took first watch while the others did their best to sleep on the floor. Ghastly chose a spot by the wall and Rapture lay down beside him. She didn't have to. She could have stayed at the other side of the room with Zeal and Stone. The fact that she came over made his heart beat a little faster and his tongue feel heavy and awkward in his mouth.

"At least your skeleton friend will be unable to roam freely while we sleep," she said softly, pulling her cloak a little tighter. The evening had brought with it an unwelcome chill.

"Not necessarily," Ghastly told her, fighting against the familiar clumsiness. "Skulduggery manages to do things the rest of us would find impossible – or, at the very least, implausible. Skeleton or not, if anyone can move undetected through this town right now, it's him."

"He sounds like a formidable person."

"He is, at that."

"He sounds like a formidable enemy."

Ghastly sighed. "He is, at that."

"Have you been friends a long time?"

"Sometimes it feels like forever," he said, and she

laughed a little, as light as summer rain. "What about you and your fellow Sisters?"

"I have only recently had the pleasure of knowing Sister Stone, but I have known Sister Zeal since I first discovered the existence of the Lady of Darkness. We earned our masks together."

"May I ask a personal question?" She gave a nod and he continued. "What made you decide that the Lady of Darkness was the god you should pray to, out of all the gods available?"

Rapture considered her answer. "Timing," she said. "She entered my life at just the right moment and suddenly the world made sense. Has that ever happened to you?"

"Not that I can think of."

"I had just lost my husband after he fell victim to a pestilence the healers could not cure. He got thinner and greyer and sicker, until there was nothing left of him except the deep lines of his face. He was a good man, though not very funny, which was a shame. A sense of humour can bring a lot to a marriage."

"I would imagine."

"I loved him, though, even if it wasn't a love they

would write poems about. It was a simple love, and quiet, enough so that when he died I was bereft. That is when I passed an old man in a busy square talking about acceptance and forgiveness and a love they *do* write poems about – a love for something greater than yourself. A love for humanity."

"That is what the Lady of Darkness offers?" said Ghastly.

"If you are ready to hear her words, yes."

In the gloom of the house, she was just a shape lying there. He could make out the silhouette of her hair, of the small tufts on either side of the straps that secured the mask to her head. He couldn't even see her eyes, swallowed as they were by the darkness. But from that darkness came her voice, low and soft and rich with the secret history of a life he knew nothing about.

They talked on, into the night, sharing whispers while the others slept around them. When their conversation eased – gently, and of its own accord – her breathing turned deep and steady, and soon after he followed her into sleep.

When he woke, he rose without disturbing her, stepped outside and boosted himself up to the roof.

"Quiet night," Shudder told him, preparing to climb down.

"Good," said Ghastly.

Shudder stayed on the edge of the roof. "Is she nice?" He didn't say her name, but didn't have to.

"You heard us talking?"

He shook his head. "I saw you looking at her. I saw her looking at you."

"She's nice."

"You should find someone new," said Shudder. "You are alone too much. Anselm was wonderful, we all liked Anselm, but Anselm was six years ago."

"Seven."

"And Anselm broke your heart."

"He did not break it, and the end of our relationship wasn't his fault."

"You are too forgiving, Ghastly. You should be more like the rest of us. You should learn to hold a grudge."

Ghastly smiled. "That's served you well, has it?"

"It has made us consistent, at the very least," said Shudder. "My point remains. Anselm was wonderful and we all liked him until he left you and broke your heart, and then we all stopped liking him. Sister Rapture, on the other hand, is here, and so far she has done nothing but make you smile, so now we like her far more than we ever liked Anselm."

"And yet you do not trust Sister Rapture."

"I do not trust anyone who aligns themselves with a religious order, especially one that worships as concerning a deity as the Lady of Darkness."

"But apart from that?"

"Apart from that, I'm sure Sister Rapture is lovely."

"Anton, it occurs to me that, in all the time we have known each other, this is the most I have ever heard you speak in one go."

"Then perhaps you should ensure I have not wasted my precious words by heeding them." He went to climb down.

"Before you go," said Ghastly, "I have been, I suppose, conducting a poll of sorts."

Shudder nodded. "As to whether or not Skulduggery could restrain himself from killing Serpine at the first opportunity."

"Do you have a view?"

"I only have hope."

"Hope that he can restrain himself?"

"Hope that, whatever he chooses, it grants him a moment of peace."

Shudder climbed down off the roof, and Ghastly sat and kept watch until the sun stretched its fingers into the brightening sky.

They left the house, allowing themselves to mingle with the good people of San Gimignano. Ghastly kept his hood up to hide his face and they made it to one of the piazzas without encountering any problems. It seemed as though the plan had worked, and the army on the doorstep had successfully distracted Mevolent's soldiers. An old man sat in the middle of the piazza, on the steps of the cistern there, ignoring the maids who queued up to draw water from the well. Some of the inns and taverns that lined the square were already open for business, but nobody seemed interested in visiting.

Using the cloaking sphere, they passed the *Duomo* undetected. They knew the buildings now and so the Elementals of the group boosted everyone to the same roof they'd been on before, the one looking out over the green courtyard. There were sorcerers already down there, standing around, trying to look casual in case any mortal passed by. So far, no sign of Skulduggery or Strickent.

When the cloaking sphere realigned and the invisibility bubble withdrew, the Dead Men and the Masked Sisters had already flattened themselves to the roof, trusting Saracen to alert them if something required their attention. Ghastly lay listening to the noise of the town around them. It was a comforting reminder that, despite the stakes and the people involved, he was as much a part of the mortal world as he was of the magical. In some ways – many ways – he actually preferred the mortal world. It wasn't that it was simpler, because the mortals had their own obstacles to overcome every day, but it was, he felt, more honest. Magic subverted the rules of reality – in some cases, it rewrote them – and Ghastly was the kind of man who liked to know where he stood.

Sister Rapture lay beside him, her head resting on her folded arms and her face turned towards him. Her eyes were closed. He wondered what she looked like under the mask.

Three hours went by, and Saracen twisted the cloaking sphere. Now recharged, the bubble sprang outwards, allowing them all to get to their feet as the sorcerers in the courtyard suddenly stood a lot straighter and wiped the bored expressions from their faces.

Mevolent and his two generals emerged from the tunnel, followed by the brute carrying Mevolent's sword. They talked among themselves for a moment, and then the generals watched as their lord and master began to trace sigils in the air, leaving glowing lines of power that hovered in space, rippling slightly like heat rising off rock. Mevolent moved in a wide circle, and when the circle was complete he started on a second circle just above the first.

When that was done, he started on a third. And then a fourth.

"Sister Stone," said Ghastly, "you're the Sensitive. How long do we have to wait between Mevolent opening the Gate and realising he has to seal it closed?"

Stone didn't take her eyes off the scene below them. "I'm not the one who had the visions," she said in that slightly unusual accent of hers. It was Irish mixed with something far more exotic. "But it isn't long. No more than a minute."

Mevolent was halfway through a fifth circle when Skulduggery burst from the tunnel.

He swept his arm in a wide arc, using the air to send the soldiers reeling. He charged through them, sword hacking at whoever was closest, heading for Mevolent, but then breaking off, diverting, going instead for Serpine.

Vengeous stepped into his path, his cutlass clashing with Skulduggery's broadsword and then flashing for his head. Skulduggery blocked the blade, but Vengeous kicked at his leg, ignored the fireball that flared against his shoulder, and wrapped one arm around Skulduggery's wrists. He knocked the broadsword out of Skulduggery's grip and sent him stumbling.

Dexter made to rush to the edge of the roof, but Ghastly held him back.

Skulduggery pulled a knife from his coat and boosted himself over the heads of the soldiers, falling towards Serpine until someone pushed at the air and sent him spinning into the trunk of a tree. He landed and someone else sent an energy stream slicing through his shirt and Skulduggery gasped as a piece of a rib clattered to the ground. Vengeous grabbed him with both hands, lifted him off his feet and rammed him, head first, back into the tree trunk. Then he threw him down and the soldiers crowded round, kicking Skulduggery as he tried to get up, tried to crawl to Serpine, who was watching the whole thing with a delighted smile.

Vengeous shoved the soldiers out of his way and stomped his boot on to Skulduggery's back. He bent down, hooking his fingers beneath the hinge of Skulduggery's jaw and then, with a grunt of effort, pulled Skulduggery's head off.

Skulduggery's body went still and Vengeous turned the skull over, looked into its eye sockets, and dropped it.

And Mevolent went back to work.

Ghastly closed his eyes and forced himself to stay where he was. When he had his breathing under control, he looked again.

With each circle, the number of sigils Mevolent carved into nothingness grew fewer and fewer. It wasn't merely a series of circles he was creating – it was a sphere, roughly the size of a barrel. When he was done, he stepped back and spread his long arms and the sigils doubled, tripled in size until the sphere was twice the height of Mevolent himself. The sigils crackled, throwing out thin fingers of energy, like lightning. Ghastly didn't know exactly what he was seeing – the languages of magic were not his area of expertise – but he watched as the fingers of lightning found each other and linked up, forming a nexus at the exact centre of the sphere.

Within the sphere, the space twisted.

The lightning curled its many flickering fingers around and through that twisted space and pulled it open, drawing back its layers in all directions at once. Blue light spilled from the wound and still it widened, and the light became a sea that roiled with violent waves of energy.

The sigils faded, but the wound, *La Porta dell'Inferno*, the Gate to Hell, stayed open.

"Get into position," Ghastly said. They all moved to the edge of the roof and then stepped off. Ghastly and Ravel used the air to keep them all within the invisibility bubble and to give them a gentle landing in the courtyard, behind a line of soldiers.

Mevolent turned to one of those soldiers. "Volunteer."

The soldier went pale. "My Lord?"

"Volunteer to pass through the Gate and be changed forever by the glory of the Faceless Ones."

The soldier didn't budge, not one step, until his fellow soldiers, terrified of being volunteered in his place, shoved him forward. He went stumbling, but any flash of anger or betrayal instantly wilted under Mevolent's eye.

Licking his lips nervously, the soldier approached the Gate. With shaking hands, he took his sword from its scabbard and poked it through. He took it back and examined the steel, appearing not at all reassured by the steam that rose from the blade's tip.

He took another step, and raised the fingers of his free hand to the sea of energy. He stopped just before he touched it, and Ghastly realised that the soldier was about to defy his master. But before he could take his hand back the energy leaped to his fingers, latching on to his skin, and the soldier screamed as the energy spread down his arm. He reeled away, dropping his sword, tried to stamp out the blue flames with his other hand, but in moments he was covered, every bit of him. He fell to his knees, his inhuman screeches becoming garbled as the energy burned through his throat, and then in an instant the blue fire went out and his charred, blackened, burnt corpse collapsed in on itself.

Mevolent approached the Gate, raising his hand like he was gauging the heat from a fire, but kept his distance.

"Another few moments," Rapture said, "then he will realise his mistake and close the Gate. Once it is closed, once we are sure it is sealed forever, you can do what you want."

Ravel nodded to Shudder. "You strike first. Go for Mevolent, focus your Gist on him and do not get distracted by anything else. Hopeless, you take out Vengeous. We will keep the others busy. Saracen, once Mevolent is on his knees, it is up to you to go for his heart."

Saracen nodded, a long-bladed knife already in his grip.

Ahead of them, Mevolent dropped his hand. "This is not the power of the Faceless Ones," he announced. "This is something else. Something dangerous. We have been lied to."

Serpine raised an eyebrow. "I will personally see to it that our scholars are horribly butchered, my Lord."

His fingers drawing new sigils in the air, Mevolent said, "Baron Vengeous, alert the Teleporters to prepare to deliver our troops behind the enemy lines. A healthy slaughter may yet salvage this day."

Vengeous gave a curt bow and strode to the tunnel,

passing a soldier who had just emerged. Vengeous stopped and turned, his heavy brow furrowing.

"You," he said, "soldier. Identify yourself."

Instead of answering, the soldier dropped his sword and bolted, and Mevolent watched him come, but didn't do anything because the soldier wasn't running at him – he was running at the Gate.

Ghastly caught Strickent's expression beneath his helmet – one of exhilarated determination – and then watched him dive into the Gate, and the sea of energy swallowed him.

The soldiers stared in stunned silence. Even Mevolent seemed at a loss for words.

"I admit," Rapture said softly, "I was not expecting that to happen."

10

With everyone else looking at the Gate, at the energy churning like a storm was brewing, the slightest bit of movement caught Ghastly's attention, and he watched Skulduggery's hand inch towards his fallen skull. Gripping it by its right eye socket, the hand pulled it slowly towards its spinal column. The jaw detached itself halfway there and the hand stopped for a moment, annoyed. Then it continued, manoeuvring the skull into position. Once the skull was where it was supposed to be, the hand went back for the jaw, brought it slowly in, and fixed it into place.

Then Skulduggery looked up, made sure all of Mevolent's people had their backs to him, and got to his feet. His knife, on the other side of the courtyard, floated low to the ground, passed between the legs of a half-dozen unsuspecting soldiers until one of them noticed and turned, curious, following the knife with his eyes, as it rose up and fitted into Skulduggery's hand.

Skulduggery leaped forward, plunging the knife into the curious soldier's chest, making him cry out.

The others spun and Skulduggery moved into them, slashing with the knife and then throwing it, burying it in another soldier's chest. Immediately, the knife flew back into his hand and he kept going, slashing and stabbing and cutting, then hurling the blade into bodies and catching it when he called it back. The enemy cursed and fumbled and died, getting in each other's way, but Ghastly knew that it was only a matter of moments before they would manage to surround him, or Mevolent or Serpine or Vengeous stepped in to end this.

Ghastly pulled his axe from his belt. The other Dead Men readied their weapons.

Rapture took out her knives. "We have to wait until after Mevolent has sealed the Gate," she said. "Saving your friend should be a secondary concern to saving the world."

"Yeah," said Ghastly, and he led the charge out of the invisibility bubble.

His axe bit into the skull of an enemy soldier as Ravel used the air to clear a path for Saracen to jump into the middle of it all. Dexter's energy streams left sizzling holes through torsos, and Hopeless and Shudder made their own way in, leaving trails of broken, screaming soldiers in their wake.

A soldier with a wild beard tried swinging his sword, but Ghastly stepped in and palmed the man's elbow, stopping his swing before it had really begun, and his axe cleaved the man's leg off at the knee. Beside him, Rapture's blades found their way past chainmail and armour, sinking into pink flesh as she whirled. Sister Stone's heavy staff mashed faces and smashed bones, and Sister Zeal's shortsword proved too nimble for the soldiers to defend themselves against.

Ghastly tripped over a fallen soldier and stumbled, colliding with Skulduggery, who dragged him back to his feet in time for Ghastly to crunch the back of his axe into a big soldier's nose.

"This is all going perfectly!" Skulduggery yelled.

Ghastly grunted.

The last soldier fell, howling, and the Dead Men and the Masked Sisters turned to Mevolent. Vengeous and Serpine stood on either side of him.

With one hand, Mevolent drew his long, long sword from the sheath the brute held and pointed it at them like it weighed no more than a dried twig. "Your ancestors are calling you home," he said. "We must acquiesce to their wishes."

Skulduggery put his knife away, and his own sword drifted into his hands. "The paving stones and the walls and the archways are calling for your blood," he responded. "We must not disappoint the architecture."

The two sides had taken no more than two steps towards each other before the blue energy in the portal, which had been a churning sea, became a whirlpool of violent activity, and a figure emerged from the other side.

Strickent Abhor's clothes, dark and layered, were of a style Ghastly had never seen before. The assassin that stood here now was significantly older than when Ghastly had seen him a moment ago. His hair was greying and his once clean-shaven face was now haggard and bearded. But his skin...

Blue sigils moved across Strickent's face and neck, his arms, his chest and his legs; sigils in a language Ghastly had never seen before. They moved as if alive, crawling and writhing, with new sigils being written on his flesh whenever a space became available. His eyes glittered with the same blue.

Serpine was closest and, Serpine being Serpine, seized the opportunity to strike while Strickent remained seemingly unaware of his presence. But, before the sword thrust could be completed, Strickent hit him with a bolt of blue light. Serpine hurtled back, losing his sword and his wig.

"We will leave this to you," Mevolent said to the Dead Men, and made for the tunnel. Serpine tried to get up, tried to follow, but collapsed. Vengeous spared him a glance, and smiled as he left.

Once they had departed, Skulduggery spoke, keeping his voice low and soothing. "Strickent, do you know who I am? My name is Skulduggery Pleasant. I helped you, do you remember? We came here together. Can you understand me?"

Strickent focused his blue eyes. "Skulduggery," he said.

"Abhor, where did you go?"

A smile. "I went to heaven."

"Heaven is through that portal?"

"Heaven for some. Hell for others."

"What happened to you?"

"The Hidden God revealed himself to me," said Strickent. "He showed me the secrets of reality. He peeled back the layers." Strickent's face crumpled all of a sudden and he sagged as if he was about to collapse. "It was horrible," he whispered, tears running from those glittering blue eyes. "The quiet machinations of the universe. What lies on the other side. What waits for us." Then he straightened, smiling, the tears forgotten. "It is beautiful and wondrous and it is paradise for everyone who loves him."

"How are you feeling?"

"Happy."

"That's good," Skulduggery said. "Would you like to come with us now? We have some people, some very nice people, who would love to talk to you, just to make sure that you are well and healthy."

"Oh, I can't do that," said Strickent. "I've got a lot of work ahead of me." His eyes flickered to Serpine, lying unconscious, and, for the first time since he'd returned, Strickent blinked. "You haven't killed him. Oh, Skulduggery, you *can* kill him, you know. You should. I would let you do that. The Hidden God, he is grateful for what you have done, freeing me from those shackles, bringing me here. He would allow you one small killing."

"I shall have plenty of time to kill Serpine once we are finished here," Skulduggery said.

"Will you?" asked Strickent, somewhat sadly. "I don't think you will." Then he looked past Skulduggery, at the Masked Sisters. "I smell the followers of the Lady of Darkness."

The Sisters stepped forward.

"Strickent Abhor," said Rapture, "your Hidden God is a blight upon this world and the worlds beyond. The Lady of Darkness will bathe you in her shadow, if you let her. There is still time to save your soul."

"My soul is on fire," Strickent answered. "It burns within me even now, and it will burn forever. I offered it to the Hidden God gladly, as I will offer yours."

"Our souls are spoken for," said Zeal.

Strickent grinned. "Then the Lady of Darkness will have to speak louder."

Zeal leaped at him and Strickent avoided her shortsword, grabbed her by the throat, and tossed her into the Gate to Hell. Ghastly reached out, closing the air round Zeal's trailing hand just before it vanished, and he pulled his arms back and yanked Zeal out of the portal. She landed, unconscious, sprawling across the grass like she had not one bone in her body. Her hair was longer and her clothes were tattered. Her mask was gone, revealing delicate features on an expressionless face, and her skin was clear of the moving sigils that blighted Strickent's face.

Rapture ran to her side, started picking her up as Hopeless loosed an arrow. It struck Strickent in the chest and broke apart without piercing his skin.

"This is interesting," Skulduggery said, striding up and swinging his sword. It bounced off Strickent's neck like it had struck rock.

Dexter fired a stream of energy, but Strickent caught the stream in his palm. Dexter poured more into it, but

Strickent moved his hand suddenly and the stream rippled like a heavy rope. The ripple hit Skulduggery and exploded against his back. He was thrown forward and went rolling into Serpine.

"We should perhaps get out of here," said Ravel.

"You're not leaving," Strickent responded. "The Hidden God will not transform all of you – some are not worthy, and those he will burn – but he may change the rest. Wait until you see what he can do. Wait until you see what you will become."

A man appeared beside Skulduggery, put his hand on his shoulder and teleported him – and Serpine – to a space in among the Dead Men. Immediately, they linked up, with Stone seizing Shudder's arm and Ghastly grabbing Rapture, and then they all teleported, arriving in the Sanctuary back in Ireland.

"Get Sister Zeal to the healers," Sagacious Tome said as Cleavers came forward to shackle Serpine.

Ghastly watched Rapture escort her unconscious friend out of the room. "She will need to be watched," he said when they were gone. "When Abhor passed through the Gate, he came back changed. I fear the same may have happened to Sister Zeal."

121

"I shall see to it," said Tome, and shook his head. "I'm sorry, I should have found a way to get to you quicker."

"We are grateful you got to us at all," said Dexter.

"I was just the mode of transport," Tome said. "You should be thanking the Sensitive who saw your impending doom and convinced me to risk the journey."

Rustica Strife, broad and strong and undoubtedly the single most feared general in Meritorious's army, with hair longer than when Ghastly had seen her last, walked into the room with a smile and Ghastly wrapped her up in the fiercest of hugs.

"Mother," he said, "it is so good to see you."

11

The Dublin Sanctuary was unusually quiet, with most of the active operatives stationed in Italy, awaiting orders. The corridors were dark and cold, and Ghastly's footsteps seemed unnaturally loud. The Dead Men had been healed and they'd eaten and now they were waiting to be teleported back to San Gimignano. They congregated in the otherwise empty dining hall, sharpening their weapons at the long tables.

Sister Stone sat apart from them, leaning back against a pillar, her shoulders slumped.

Ghastly stopped beside her. "How is your friend?" he asked.

"She isn't my friend. I mean, I don't know her well enough to call her..." Stone sighed, and rubbed her face through her mask. "Physically, Zeal is fine. But those few seconds in the portal... they converted her. All she talks about, when she does talk, is the Hidden God. She's abandoned the Lady of Darkness. Abandoned her whole life."

"Perhaps there remains a way to get her back," said Ghastly. "Perhaps there is a cure."

Stone gave the smallest of shrugs, humouring him more than anything, and Meritorious walked in.

"Serpine is still alive, I take it?" the Grand Mage asked.

"Alive and chained up in the dungeon," said Ravel, "where he belongs."

Skulduggery finished sharpening his knife, and put it away. "Serpine belongs dead."

"He undoubtedly does, my friend," said Meritorious, "but not until we have prised every last secret from his mind. While he is still useful to us, he remains breathing. That is an order."

"So long as I get to be the one prising those secrets, I see no reason to rush his death," Skulduggery responded, shrugging. "He didn't rush mine, after all."

"Tell me now," said Meritorious, "about the change that has come over Strickent Abhor."

They all looked to Sister Rapture. She hesitated, her eyes flickering to Ghastly's, and then she began to undo her mask. As her fingers worked the knots loose, he realised he didn't especially care what she looked like. So long as she had a face, so long as there wasn't a void beneath the mask with two eyes floating in it, it truly didn't matter if she was beautiful or plain. The straps fell open and she folded the mask into her hands. Her face was slender, her cheekbones high, and she had a flurry of freckles across her nose. Her top lip was thin, the bottom one plump, both cracked after spending all that time behind a mask. She was unsmiling as she spoke.

"The Hidden God transformed him, and he transformed our sister, Zeal, imbuing them with his power. We don't know what discipline of magic they wield if, indeed, they wield any that we would recognise. The Hidden God is a mystery to us."

"I thought your god and Abhor's god were enemies," said Dexter.

"The Lady of Darkness views no one or no thing as her enemy. How any other gods view her, however, is not within her power to control."

"We need to know what you know," Meritorious told her, "no matter how meagre that may be. You wanted us to ensure that Mevolent both widened and then sealed the Gate to Hell. We failed in that task and so we will fix our mistake, but we need to know what will happen now that the Gate is active."

"Our Sensitives tell us that Strickent will continue to draw strength from it. He will grow ever more powerful – as, I imagine, will Zeal – though our Sensitives failed to warn us of the threat to her."

"Can Mevolent still seal the Gate?" asked Shudder.

Rapture paused, and glanced at Stone, who nodded.

"Yes," said Rapture.

"Then we have to tell him of the danger we all face," Shudder said. "We must work with him."

Ghastly frowned. "Work with Mevolent? Are you mad? We have been trying to kill each other for over a hundred years!"

"Anton is right," Meritorious said. "If Mevolent is the only one with the knowledge and power to do what needs to be done, there is no other choice. An accommodation must be reached."

"An accommodation," Skulduggery murmured.

"I understand that this will be difficult for many of you to accept."

"The first thing Mevolent is going to ask for," Skulduggery said, "is Serpine back."

"Most likely."

"We are not giving Serpine back."

"Strickent Abhor and his Hidden God pose a greater threat to—"

"*We are not giving Serpine back!*" Skulduggery roared.

The dining hall fell silent.

Meritorious spoke calmly. "From what I understand, if the Gate to Hell remains open, Strickent Abhor will be able to convert more innocent people into followers of the Hidden God. Time passes differently on the other side of the Gate, am I correct? Abhor was there for a scant few minutes and came back older and stronger. Sister Zeal was not in there for mere moments, but was changed all the same. If years pass in minutes, Abhor could recruit a seasoned army of fanatics with access to powers we do not yet understand, much less are ready to defend against. The Gate must be closed. We need Mevolent to do this. All other considerations are secondary."

Skulduggery watched him. If he had anything to say in response, it was lost when Mr Bliss walked in, his cloak twisted over one shoulder, his boots splattered with mud.

"My friend," said Meritorious, going to meet him, "thank you for coming so quickly."

They conversed quietly for a few moments, and then Meritorious left the hall and Bliss came over. He removed his cloak, used it to rub the back of his bald head, which was, Ghastly saw now, dotted with someone's blood.

"We intend to meet and parley with Mevolent," Bliss said, dropping his cloak on the table. "I understand there are no objections to this."

No one objected. Even Skulduggery stayed silent.

"Once the threat posed by Strickent Abhor has been dealt with, we will need to immediately shift our attention to Mevolent and Vengeous. This will be their approach when dealing with us. They will attack at the earliest opportunity, so we have to strike before that. Hopeless,

Baron Vengeous will be your target. Your job will not be to arrest him, apprehend him, or otherwise take him into custody. He must be killed."

Hopeless nodded.

"The rest of you will be going after Mevolent. As will I. As will every sorcerer in the vicinity. Once Vengeous is dead, Hopeless will also join us in this endeavour. Killing Mevolent is our priority, no matter who else has to die, or how many."

"And Serpine?" Skulduggery asked. "In order to parley, Mevolent will want Serpine returned."

"And we acquiesce," said Bliss.

"That is a mistake."

"And, because it *is* a mistake, Mevolent will expect us to make more of them. If he has one flaw, Mevolent believes himself superior to all others. This causes him to underestimate his enemy. We will indulge him in this folly until it suits us to behave otherwise. That is not to say, however, that this is a mistake we embrace without some insurance."

He took a bundle from his pocket, laid it on his open palm and carefully peeled back the cloth to reveal a golden bracelet.

"Before we hand Serpine over, you will put this on his wrist – explain it away as being an additional binding to his magic. You can remove it when you remove his shackles – at such time, its poison will already have entered his system. Fatal, slow to take effect, but agonising once it does. There is no cure. Do not let this come into contact with the skin of anyone you do not want to die."

Skulduggery took the bracelet from the cloth in Bliss's palm, and slipped it into his coat.

12

The meeting with Mevolent was set for noon the next day.

While Meritorious and his generals arranged security and planned counter-attacks, in case Mevolent chose this ideal moment to wipe out the Grand Mage of the Irish Sanctuary, Ghastly and the Dead Men spent the morning guarding Nefarian Serpine.

Skulduggery couldn't bring a knife, a sword, or any form of heavy object anywhere close to the man who'd murdered his family. One of the other guards must have let Serpine in on what was transpiring because that smug, arrogant grin had returned to his face. He goaded Saracen through the bars of his cell, taunted Shudder, insulted Hopeless. None of them responded with anything more than a bored expression.

Serpine didn't goad Skulduggery, not even when he entered his cell to secure the poisoned bracelet upon his wrist. Skulduggery was different. While Skulduggery appeared perfectly in control, his voice calm and deep and measured, it was as if his very soul was vibrating with violent rage. Ghastly could feel it on the air. It was almost contagious, this rage. It made him want to barge into the cell and tear Serpine apart himself – though Ghastly had been wanting to do that for the last thirteen years, so not much had changed there.

The Dead Men stood around Skulduggery in case he attempted to throttle Serpine to death right there and then and ruin any chance they had of getting the Gate sealed shut. But Skulduggery left the cell without incident and then went to sit in the darkness of the dungeon.

Rapture and Stone, having checked on Zeal's well-being and come away disheartened, joined them down there. Stone sat alone, her face hidden by the mask.

Rapture stood with Ghastly at the far side of the dungeon, away from Serpine's cell, leaning against one of the pillars. She had a kind smile and warm, intelligent eyes.

"So it was your mother who arranged for the Teleporter last night?" Rapture said. "Does she have a habit of saving your life?"

"She does," Ghastly replied. "It's an innate skill that she has never lost, thank God. As a Sensitive, she has seen visions of my death a dozen times and she has managed to avert each one. So far anyway."

"That is an incredibly useful parent to have. Neither my mother nor my father were gifted with magic. I watched them grow old and die, and then I watched my sisters and my brothers grow old and die, and when their children began to grow old I couldn't take it any more. The mage's curse, is that not what they say? Is your father magical also?"

Ghastly nodded. "A healer, and still with my mother, all these centuries later."

She smiled. "That is lovely."

"He taught me everything I know about being a tailor. I was apprenticed at our family workshop, but, really, I had already learned so much simply by being around him. He developed a new system of armouring clothes and swore me to secrecy over it."

"Is that what you do when you are not fighting in this war?"

"That is what I want to get back to, yes. You?"

"I like to paint," she said, and blinked, surprised. "I have never told anyone that before."

"You have never told anyone that you are an artist?"

"It has always been my little secret, a part of me that I never felt the need to share."

"Why did you tell me?"

"I sincerely do not know," she said, and laughed. "But I think calling me an artist is, perhaps, an indulgence too far. I was never very good at expressing myself with words, although I have improved over the years, but with paint, with charcoal, with pencil... I am able to be who I am."

"And who is that?"

"If I could tell you with words, I would not need to paint."

She smiled at him and he smiled back.

"Is your father involved in the war?" she asked.

"No," said Ghastly. "Fighting has always been my

mother's domain. Honestly, my father is not in the best of health. He seems to catch everything. Every plague and fever and pox that sweeps through a country. A lot of ailments, he can rid himself of, but his own healers tell us he has a different sickness, a blood sickness that they do not know how to treat."

"And it is serious?"

"Some Sensitives cannot foresee the futures of some people close to them – whether this block is magical or merely of the mind, nobody knows – and my father is one such person to my mother. She does, however, know some of the best Sensitives in the world, and none of them can see a future for him beyond three years."

"But that is no time at all."

"We are hoping the healers will find a way to help him. Doctors are discovering new solutions to old problems all the time, using magic or science or roots and flowers from far-off places."

"I quite like that idea," said Rapture. "I would love my life to be saved by a flower."

Sagacious Tome stepped into the dungeon and nodded to Ghastly and Saracen. It was time.

*

The tent was the size of a dining hall, and, though it sat within an arrow's flight of San Gimignano's southern entrance, it was hidden from mortal eyes by a system of cloaking spheres and complicated sigils that someone like Ghastly wasn't meant to understand. He was a simple man who understood simple things – politics and invisibility were not among them.

When Mevolent entered the tent, the temperature dropped, despite the warmth of the day. There was a coldness to the man that wasn't caused by mere intimidation: his mastery of Elemental magic allowed him to control the temperature of his immediate surroundings. Not even Eachan Meritorious could do that.

If the Grand Mage was awed in Mevolent's presence, he gave no sign. He greeted him curtly, never taking his eyes off him, not even to glance at Vengeous or the warriors they'd brought with them. He left that to Ghastly and Shudder and Saracen.

Mevolent surveyed them, surveyed the tent, and did not speak. A nasty little man hurried up to his side, but stayed half a step back. The Voice was clad in a black cloak. His hair was long and lank and his skin seeped with oil and pus from broken blisters. He was a man who smelled like he was rotting from the inside.

"Serpine is not here," the Voice said. For a man chosen to speak for Mevolent, the Voice's own voice curdled in his throat.

"Serpine will remain as our guest," said Meritorious, "until we have reached an accord."

"That is not the agreement we arrived at," the Voice responded, sneering, showing black gums. "You were to give him to us as an appeasement, to engender our goodwill. The Lord Mevolent's goodwill has not been engendered."

Meritorious raised an eyebrow. "If I have hurt your feelings, Mevolent, you have my unreserved apology – but we have more important matters to discuss."

The Voice tittered. "How can we be expected to discuss important matters if we cannot even trust you to fulfil your first promise to us?"

"You'll get Serpine back when I am happy with how things have progressed."

"The game you play is dangerous," said the Voice,

"but you are lucky. The Lord Mevolent likes dangerous games."

Ghastly's eyes moved from Mevolent to Vengeous and back again.

"Strickent Abhor is the man who emerged from the Gate to Hell," Meritorious said. "He claims to have been transformed by the Hidden God. From what we understand, the longer that portal stays open, the more powerful he will become."

"And you are here," said the Voice, "to beg the Lord Mevolent to close it for you."

"No one here is begging. This will affect you just as much as it will affect us."

Another titter. "The Lord Mevolent doubts that very much."

"Abhor is recruiting an army as we stand here. It may very well be only a matter of time before his followers outnumber yours and ours combined."

"Then attack him," said the Voice. "Sally forth. By your own words, you have not time to waste."

"And once we attack him, and we lose, what are you going to do? Saunter in and finish him off while he is tired? That will not happen, Mevolent. Our Sensitives have told us so, which means your Sensitives have told you the same. Once he has done with us, he will go after you, and you will fall."

"No," the Voice said. "There is a difference between us, old man. You will be fighting alone, whereas we will have the Faceless Ones at our backs."

"And where are they? Are they hiding, perhaps? Waiting for the perfect moment to reveal themselves? Your gods, if they even exist, if they are even still alive, are lost to you. But the Hidden God is not lost. The Hidden God is through that portal. The Gate to Hell leads straight to him."

The Voice said nothing.

Then Mevolent spoke. "You propose an alliance."

"We do," said Meritorious. "We send a team in – the Dead Men, plus an equal number of your finest warriors, and at least two Teleporters. Once they clear the way to the Gate, you close it and seal the portal forever. Abhor will still have his power, but he won't grow any stronger. He can be dealt with, the same way we deal with any of our enemies."

"We have no time for sneaking," said the Voice. "It is better to use the full force of our armies to crush this

Strickent Abhor before the number of his followers grows."

Meritorious shook his head. "If we send in our armies, mortals will die."

"And?"

"The mortals must not die."

"It would appear to the Lord Mevolent that this is a problem for you, and not one for the Lord Mevolent."

"The mortals must not die," Meritorious repeated.

The Voice sighed. "This plan of yours – the Lord Mevolent takes all the risk."

"That's the unfortunate consequence of being the only one powerful enough to see that the job is done."

"And when do you propose we send this team in, old man?"

"Tonight, under cover of darkness."

"We meet again," Mevolent said. "Here, at sundown. We bring our warriors; you bring yours."

"Very well," said Meritorious, but Mevolent was already walking out of the tent.

The Voice was the last to leave. He tilted his head. "And you will bring General Serpine."

"Of course."

13

Trying to wrangle a moment alone alone with his mother was proving to be a task beyond the meagre abilities of Ghastly Bespoke.

Every few minutes, there would be some new decision that Rustica Strife had to make or be a part of or be told about. Sorcerers sought her counsel and her power, and often both at the same time. After waiting an hour instead of the agreed-upon five minutes, Ghastly went looking, eventually finding her laughing with, of all people, Skulduggery, down by the dungeons.

"We have been talking about you," Rustica said, grinning widely as Ghastly approached. "It seems there are stories you have yet to tell me – specifically a story about a polar bear and a fox?"

Ghastly glared at his friend. "Of all the stories you could have mentioned, why that one?"

"It's the funniest," Skulduggery said.

"I failed to find it funny at the time and I struggle to find it funny even now."

"That is only because your sense of humour tends to vanish when you lose your trousers."

Rustica laughed and clapped her hands. "Another story in which you lose your trousers? They should write songs about you, my son!"

"Could I have some time alone with my mother, Skulduggery? Is that too much to ask?"

"I'm afraid it is," Rustica said before Skulduggery could answer, "for we have matters to deal with." She started walking, and they dutifully kept pace. "The Masked Sisters are hiding something," she told them. "I don't know what it is, exactly, and I don't know the danger they pose – but they are hiding their true motivations for all of this."

"We can trust them," said Ghastly. "We can trust Rapture, at least."

Rustica gave him a look. "And why is it that you trust her in particular?"

He did his very best not to blush. "She has proven herself. She's fought alongside us."

"Just because Strickent Abhor and his Hidden God are her enemies does not mean she is our friend. Do not be fooled by kind smiles and flattering words, my son."

"I am not being fooled by anything, Mother. I like to think I am a good judge of character."

"Is that so?" she said, amused. "Skulduggery, what do you think of my boy's skills in judging character?"

"I do not rate his skills too highly," Skulduggery answered. "I am his best friend, after all."

Ghastly frowned at him. "Are you saying I should not trust you?"

"Of course you shouldn't. I appreciate the trust that you have in me – I really do – but I am also, quite honestly, flabbergasted and appalled at your naivety. There are times when I doubt that I can truly trust myself. When all of these current crises are over, assuming any of us survive, you and I are going to have a long talk about the pitfalls of unwavering and unthinking trust."

"Sometimes I just do not know how to talk to you," Ghastly said, shaking his head. "And as for you, Mother—"

"As for me?"

"—I trust Rapture because I believe that she is a good person – but that doesn't mean she is not keeping secrets. If you believe she is hiding something, we need to find out what it is."

"Then a confrontation is in order," Rustica said, the grin returning. "Oh, I do so *love* a good confrontation."

Ghastly called the rest of the Dead Men together and they met with Morwenna Crow, and together they found the Masked Sisters sitting at a table in the empty dining hall. Sister Stone had removed her mask now, too, and they were talking quietly, faces pensive. Stone was pretty, with a serious set to her jaw, though she shared little of Rapture's warmth.

Rustica stood with the Dead Men while Crow sat at the table.

"Elder Crow," Rapture said, somewhat warily, "has there been a change of plans?"

"No change," said Crow. "Not yet anyway. We thought we might take this opportunity, before everyone plunges into danger yet again, to perhaps have a talk. You came to us with dire warnings of what would happen if Strickent Abhor succeeded in assassinating Mevolent. You spoke of Nefarian Serpine and Baron Vengeous continuing Mevolent's plan and, with a lot of effort and a significant amount of time, eventually managing to widen the Gate to Hell themselves, but lacking the power to close it again. You told us what that would look like, the effect it would have on the world. The warnings you gave us, confirmed by our own Sensitives, were of such dreadful magnitude that we agreed with your assessment that we should do everything within our power to prevent Abhor from killing Mevolent.

"And that is what we did – and yet we seem to have arrived at the same point. The Gate has been widened, the power is escaping and Abhor appears to have become the Hidden God's Herald on Earth. If anything, the situation we are currently in is worse than it would have been if we had done nothing."

"Not so," said Rapture. "At least Mevolent is alive. He can still close the Gate. I realise things have not gone according to plan, Elder Crow, and I apologise, but when trying to divert the river of destiny, one must be prepared for things to get... muddy."

Crow smiled, and nodded. "We know all about muddy, Sister Rapture. And this river of destiny, as you so eloquently put it, is indeed a difficult river to divert. Unpredictability is as much a part of that riverbed as silt and sand. But we have a plan, do we not? An alliance with Mevolent. Half of our Sensitives tell us not to trust him, and half tell us we have no choice. Such is our lot, it would seem. So what are you not telling us?"

Rapture paled. "I'm sorry?"

"There is something you're not telling us. I do not need our Sensitives to tell me when someone has a secret – we all have secrets, do we not? But it would seem to me that the secret you hold might be of great importance to the rest of us, so I think you should unburden yourself of it here and now."

"Or we could instead address the person making all the decisions," Skulduggery said, his head tilting, "and ask Sister Stone why she is lying to us."

Ghastly didn't like to see it but, amazingly, Rapture went even paler.

"I have seniority," she said. "I am in charge of—"

Sister Stone put a hand on Rapture's arm as she got slowly to her feet – slow enough as to not cause undue alarm. "It's OK, Sister," she said. "We've been found out."

The Dead Men watched her carefully, and Ghastly readied himself for an attack.

"We haven't been lying to you," Stone said, "but we have been keeping secrets. I would apologise, but the secrets were necessary. At least, I thought they were. Now I'm not so sure. This is all wrong. Nothing is working out the way it should. I don't know what's happening, but then I'm not the expert. I get sent to sort out problems. That's what I do. I hit things until they stop working, and I break things until they get fixed."

Dexter frowned. "This is the first time I have really heard you speak for longer than a few words," he said. "Where is that accent from? It's Irish but... not Irish."

"I can explain the accent, don't worry. I can explain everything." She took a deep breath. "Let's start with my name. I'm not Sister Stone. I'm not one of the Masked Sisters, and I'm not, technically, a follower of the Lady of Darkness. My name is Valkyrie Cain. I'm from the future."

14

"Wow," the woman called Valkyrie said, "this must be one of those pregnant silences I've been hearing about. Do you think they call them that because they're heavy and expectant, or because once they're done they give birth to a whole slew of little baby words? Probably both, right? Man, I'm smart."

No one said anything. It was, in truth, difficult to think of something worthwhile to say. Ghastly looked at her again, this woman from the future. Tall and broad-shouldered and strong, pretty and dark-haired and powerful, but where before he had thought her grim and pensive, now she looked positively relaxed, as if she had shrugged off a weight that had been resting on those shoulders. She actually smiled as she looked round at them.

"You're from the future?" Crow said tentatively.

"That's right," said Valkyrie. "I'm from the twenty-first century. It's amazing there. We have jetpacks and flying cars and robot butlers. Everything is brilliant and we've eradicated world hunger and solved the climate crisis. It's great. You'll love it."

She spoke English fluently – though Dexter was right, she had an accent that didn't quite convince as Irish – but the words she used, or at least the arrangement of them, were somewhat jarring to listen to.

"Time-travel is impossible," said Dexter.

"It is," Valkyrie agreed, "until it isn't."

"Miss Cain..." said Crow.

"Call me Valkyrie, please. We're all friends here. Or most of us are anyway. Or most of us will be, at any rate."

"Valkyrie, do you have proof that you're from the future?"

She spread her arms wide. "Ask me anything. Ask me who the American president is, who the British prime minister is, who our own Taoiseach is, who won the Second World War, what the gross domestic product of Finland is – anything."

Shudder frowned. "What is the gross domestic product of Finland?"

Valkyrie made a face. "I don't know. Sorry. I don't even know why I suggested that. It's just something you learn in school, for some reason."

"Wait, wait," said Saracen, "there are going to be *two* world wars?"

"Yeah, everyone loved the first one so much they decided to make a sequel. Spoiler. Actually, wait. Originally, I wasn't supposed to tell you anything about the future, but things have already changed here, in my past, and yet I'm still here talking to you, so maybe it doesn't matter? Is that what I'm saying...? I don't know. It's tricky. I'm not a time-traveller, you know?"

"But you are a time-traveller," Skulduggery said.

"Well, yes," she said, "I am, obviously, but I'm only a time-traveller in the technical sense – I'm not a *natural* time-traveller."

"Valkyrie," Crow said, "I'm still waiting for proof that you are from where you say you are."

"Yeah. But how do I prove that? Do you want me to sing something from my time? No, that's dumb. Also, the moment I said that, my mind went blank. Now the only song in my head is 'You Spin Me Round' by those guys with the hair, but that's from back in the 1980s. Which, admittedly, for you, is still the future, but for me it's so retro, you know? Ah, dammit, it's really in my head now. It's pushing everything else out."

Crow glanced at Rustica. "Would you take a peek to see if she's lying?"

"Good idea," Valkyrie said. "And I won't resist, I promise. Just don't go too deep, OK? There are some things you really shouldn't know."

"Some things *I* shouldn't know specifically," Rustica said, "or some things *we* shouldn't know collectively?"

"A little bit of both."

Rustica gazed at Valkyrie, eyes narrowing ever so slightly, and then she nodded at Crow. "I can sense no subterfuge. She is either telling the truth, or she believes she is."

"Very well," said Crow. "Valkyrie, I think you should tell us what you can, don't you?"

"Thank you," Valkyrie said. She stepped back, looked

at them all, scowled at Ravel for some reason, and took a deep breath. "OK then. To get this out of the way, I'm not like the rest of you. I'm not restricted to one type of magic, and I'm not restricted to only the *known* types of magic. Among other abilities, I can latch on to people's powers, I'm something of a Sensitive, and I can see people's auras. I can also fly and shoot lightning of varying colours, but that's just me showing off. So there I was, in the future, being all cool and stuff, with everybody loving me, and I get this vision of Strickent Abhor."

"The Lady of Darkness spoke to her," said Rapture.

"Well," Valkyrie said, "did she? Or did I just have a vision?"

"You had a vision because the Lady of Darkness allowed you to have one."

"Let's leave that there. But, however it happened, I saw what Strickent was up to."

"And what was he up to?" Skulduggery asked.

"Right at that moment, in my present and your future, he was stabbing an old man."

"Strickent is a time-traveller, too?"

"Oh, yeah, sorry – should have opened with that.

Here's the story." She started to pace as she talked. "The Gate to Hell was discovered in 1583 by a guy called Tithonus. Tithonus was a perfectly ordinary mortal who just happened to notice something weird one day as he was taking a new short cut to wherever. He walked through the spot where the Gate opens, and he felt it bubbling with energy. Most people would just frown and walk on, but Tithonus hung around. The thing about the Gate is that, even before Mevolent widened it, it was still technically open. The very fact that it could be noticed meant it could be touched. What do perfectly ordinary mortals do when they notice something weird like that?"

"They touch it," said Skulduggery.

"They touch it, exactly, because perfectly ordinary mortals are not very bright. Tithonus poked and prodded this seemingly empty space until he poked it at just the right angle. The energy hurt him quite badly – his arm was terribly burned – but he wasn't killed. He couldn't be killed. Since that day in 1583, Tithonus got older, sure, but he hasn't been able to die. He hasn't been able to leave town, either, without experiencing agonising pain that no drugs or magical solution can even begin to help. Today, here in 1703, he is a hundred and forty-two years old and probably looks every bit of it. He's still alive in my time, too, where he's over four hundred and sixty years old and is a crumbling, mumbling old dude who is so bored with this town it's unreal.

"So, in my time, the Hidden God led Strickent to Tithonus and Strickent cut him. I'll get to why in a moment. In my vision, I saw the knife he used, and I saw the sigil carved on to the blade. This being a magic thing, naturally we decided to give the knife a fancy name, because fancy names are everything, so we're calling it the Unix Blade."

Saracen looked worried. "The Eunuch Blade?"

"Unix," said Valkyrie.

"Eunuchs?"

"See, I said this would happen. I said people would think we're saying eunuchs."

"But you're definitely not saying eunuchs?"

"Definitely not."

"What is a unix?" asked Ghastly.

"I was told that it's a system for describing a point in time, so that's what we're..." Valkyrie shook her head. "Listen, I didn't choose it, I didn't want it and I certainly didn't vote for it. Then I was told this wasn't a vote and I was to put my hand down, but the point is, I can't be blamed for the stupid and confusing name. Apparently, though, and I didn't know this until recently, there is a Eunuch Blade already out there in the world somewhere."

Saracen went pale. "There is?"

"In a way," Shudder murmured, "aren't *all* blades Eunuch Blades?"

"Can we please return to the subject?" asked Crow, growing irritated. "Valkyrie, please continue."

Valkyrie nodded. "Right. Sorry. So our resident expert on sigils figured out that the sigil on the Unix Blade was designed to mark Tithonus throughout his life, meaning that Strickent could find and track Tithonus at any point from the moment he touched the Gate in 1583 to the moment of his theoretical death at some stage in my future. The Hidden God then gave Strickent a blast of power that sent him back in time."

"And Strickent used the Unix Blade to find Tithonus here and now," Skulduggery said.

"That's correct. The way it was explained to me was that Strickent was thrown off a cliff, but the rope he held was secured to a point halfway down. That point was Tithonus, and this allowed Strickent to swing in and grab on to the ledge at the exact moment when Mevolent was going to widen the Gate, realise the danger it posed and seal it forever. All he had to do was either kill Mevolent before he did anything at all, which would have been easier, or interrupt him before he sealed it, which would have been better, because then the Gate would have been widened, but trickier to manage."

"And that's what he managed."

"Yes."

"So you were sent back to prevent this from happening," Ghastly said. "Why you?"

"I'm the only one who can time-travel," Valkyrie answered. She took a skull made of dark metal from her pocket, pressed it to her chest and tapped it. A black material flowed over her body. When it was done, she pulled up the hood and then tugged a white, angular skull mask down over her face. "This is a modified necronaut suit," she said. "Elder Crow, you'd be familiar with this, wouldn't you?"

"I'm familiar with other necronaut suits," said Crow, "but nothing quite like that."

Valkyrie pulled up the mask and tapped the metal

skull and the suit flowed away again. Ghastly had to stop himself from asking after whoever had designed the mechanism. "Like I said, it's modified. There was a man, Destrier, who had been working on a way to travel through time. He'd infused another suit with his power, and we managed to transfer some of that energy to mine."

"And then," Skulduggery said, "because you can latch on to other people's magic..."

"I kick-started it and travelled back to now," Valkyrie finished, nodding. "And because I'd, I suppose, *internalised* that power to a degree, I could walk around without the suit covering me and not, y'know, be flung back to my own time. I had to disguise myself so you wouldn't recognise me in the future when we actually meet, and I didn't want Strickent realising I'd followed him back, so I made contact with the Masked Sisters and explained the situation."

"She told us that the Lady of Darkness had sent her," said Rapture.

Valkyrie laughed and made a face, rocking her hand back and forward, like a pair of scales. "I told them she *may* have set me on my path. Who knows, right? Anyway,

Rapture and Zeal agreed to accompany me, and here we are."

"So you came back to save the world," said Ravel, "and now everything is going wrong?"

"First of all," Valkyrie said, "shut up. Second of all, not everything is going wrong. Most things are going wrong, yes, but that's to be expected. After all, before something can go right, it first has to go wrong."

"That's not true," said Hopeless.

"That's not true at all," said Dexter.

"Well, that's always been my experience," Valkyrie said, clearly getting annoyed. "The point is, this is time-travel, so changes are to be expected. In my timeline, the original timeline, this whole Gate to Hell thing didn't get nearly so much attention. Most of you stayed doing whatever you were doing before this, and, by the time you heard about what was going on, the Gate was already closed and the danger had passed. So, yeah, there will be some ripples throughout time that, apparently, time itself will sort out before they reach the future. That's one of the theories anyway. It's a whole thing about the universe correcting itself. I really hope that's true because... I mean, if it isn't, then I don't know what kind of future I'll be going back to."

"So your mission," Skulduggery said, "is to cause as little disruption as possible? Even though the very act of telling us that time-travel will someday be achieved would be classed as disruptive in and of itself."

"Oh, don't worry – this moment has been taken into account. The future version of you sat me down and told me, with absolute confidence, that you, your future self's past self, would be able to figure this all out long before I had to tell you. So did you?"

"Did I figure out that you travelled here from the future?" Skulduggery asked. "No, I did not."

Valkyrie gave a little smile. "So you're not quite as smart as you think you are."

"On the other hand," Skulduggery said, "my future self telling you this would have planted the idea in your head that I *would* figure it out, thus lowering your inhibitions about us discovering the truth and leaving the way open for this very conversation in which you tell us everything you have just told us."

The smile vanished, replaced with a scowl. "God, you're annoying."

"We are friends, then, in the future?"

Valkyrie struggled to maintain the scowl, but it was a losing battle. "Yes," she said. "We're very close friends."

Saracen raised an eyebrow. "Are you friends with the rest of us?"

"Some of you, absolutely."

"Are all of us still alive in your time?" asked Hopeless.

Valkyrie didn't answer immediately, and the room filled slowly with a soft chorus – *ooooh* – and then laughter.

"Don't worry," Ghastly told her, "we all know we are going to get ourselves killed at some stage."

"It's almost reassuring," said Dexter.

"What does it mean," said Shudder, "that Valkyrie's past – our present – is now set on a different course? Surely events can no longer play out as before?"

"I do not know," Crow said. "I will have to consult with the Grand Mage and seek out some informed opinions. This is all very intriguing." Shadows pooled around her as she stood and when they dispersed she was gone.

"Tell us more about the future," said Saracen.

"Do not," Shudder said, a stern edge to his voice.

"We cannot risk contaminating the timeline any more than we already have done."

"I don't want specifics," Saracen responded. "I just want general information. What do people do for fun?"

Valkyrie grinned. "All kinds of things. We watch TV, which is kind of like watching a play on a piece of glass, and you can take the glass wherever you go."

"That must be cumbersome."

"Actually, you can fit it in your pocket."

Saracen frowned. "So are the actors really small, or just really far away?"

"It's recorded. Like an Echo Stone, sort of. We also play games where we control, like, little drawings of people that move around and do what we tell them."

"Like reflections?"

"Sort of. Not really. We can do all this stuff on our phones, which are devices we use to communicate, and we can speak to people on the other side of the world and listen to music and, again, play games. There was a game called *Angry Birds* that everyone used to play, but I don't know anyone who plays it any more."

"Why are they angry?" Shudder asked. "Do birds not fare well in the future?"

"They're only drawings of birds – but real birds... I mean, yeah, they're not doing too great. Very few things are, to be honest. People are messing things up wherever they go. Mortal civilisation has become more industrialised and so much better in some ways, but so much worse in a lot of others."

"Have the sorcerers not stepped in?" Ravel asked.

"The Sanctuaries don't interfere in the mortal world," Valkyrie said, her tone growing sharper.

Ravel nodded gently. "Have I done something to upset you, Valkyrie? Either now or in the future?"

"I think it's safe to say you've upset me, yes."

"In that case, while I do not know what it is I did, I do apologise."

"I want to know about your accent," said Dexter. "Where are you from?"

"I'm from Ireland, but I was exposed to a lot of American TV and movies as a kid," she said. "Add that to the fact that language and accents evolve naturally anyway and this is just how I talk. The world is a lot more, I don't know... closer, in some ways, I suppose. Because things are more immediate, and communication and travel and work and life are so fast and interconnected, I suppose things like accents and ethnicities have melted together, you know?"

"It sounds lovely," said Ghastly.

"It has its moments."

As the others peppered Valkyrie with questions, Rapture stepped up to Ghastly. "I owe you an apology."

Her voice was so quiet, he had to lean in to hear her. He liked leaning in. He liked getting close to her.

"You do?"

"I kept the truth of our mission from you," she said. "From all of you."

"Oh." He was unsure how to respond. "And are you apologising to all of us?"

"No," she said, after a moment. "Just to you."

He smiled at her. He'd never smiled so easily before. "You kept a secret you had to keep. It's a secret I would have kept, too, if I were in your position. A good secret. You do not owe me anything."

"I feel like I do, however."

"In that case," he said, "apology accepted."

"Thank you."

She remained where she was for a moment, as if she was trying to think of something else to say. He wished she would. It occurred to him that he could fill this gap himself and so he scrambled for the words, but nothing he thought of sounded natural in his mind, and so she smiled again and walked back to Valkyrie and something occurred to Ghastly, something that took him by surprise.

It was her. He'd been waiting on someone, someone to drink his fill of, to drown himself in. After a lifetime of searching, he'd found her. She had come to him in the hills of Tuscany, hidden behind a mask and secrets.

She reached Valkyrie and glanced back and it was there and it was then, in that single glance, that drew him forward that final step, and he fell in love.

15

Drestan Bizarre was a man most unsuited to being a member of the Council of Elders, and this reason alone meant he would probably have been Ghastly's favourite anyway, even without the history they shared. As an active member of the magical community, Ghastly shared histories with many people, but few could claim to be quite so formative. It had been Drestan whom Ghastly had followed into battle as a young man. It had been Drestan who had introduced both Ghastly and Skulduggery to the more esoteric side of magic. It had been Drestan who had taught them the value of disobeying orders.

It was, indeed, fair to say that, without Drestan Bizarre, Ghastly Bespoke and Skulduggery Pleasant would not be the people they were today.

Ghastly found the most unlikely of Elders in the most unlikely of places: sitting behind his desk in his own office chamber.

"I don't think I have ever seen you in here," Ghastly said, stepping through the doorway as hot flame flickered over cold stone walls.

Too handsome, too pale, too tired, Drestan closed the book he'd been frowning at and sat back in his chair, smiling at his protégé. "I try not to make a habit of visiting this place – I might get too comfortable and lose my taste for wandering."

"Comfortable," Ghastly echoed, looking around. "Didn't there used to be cushions in here?"

"Others need cushions more than I." Drestan's face turned serious. "I have been told that Skulduggery is in the vicinity of a certain arch-enemy, and that he has managed not to kill him yet. Has he finally discovered how to control his temper?"

"I would not presume to go quite so far as that," Ghastly responded, "but he has shown definite improvements. In truth, it is a struggle for the rest of us not to tear Serpine limb from limb ourselves."

"I would imagine being across the table from him would be a battle against one's own instincts."

"And we were across the table from not just Serpine, but Mevolent himself," said Ghastly. "I'm surprised you were not part of our delegation."

Drestan looked annoyed. "The Grand Mage decided that having all three Irish Elders sitting directly opposite the most powerful sorcerer alive would not be the best of ideas. Which is why I am here, safe within the Sanctuary, while my fellows are preparing to spar and joust – if only with words – with the enemy. Sometimes I think it was a mistake to accept this post. Other times I know it was." He shifted in his seat. "But enough about my woes, my friend. You come here seeking advice."

Ghastly blinked. "I do?"

"Of course. You always come seeking advice, as does Skulduggery. The difference between you is that you actually take my advice when I give it, something

Skulduggery has never quite managed. This, by the way, endears me to you immensely, and means you are by far my favourite."

Ghastly laughed. "Thank you. I am honoured."

"As you should be. So what troubles you?"

"One of the Masked Sisters – Sister Rapture – has been of great use to us so far in this endeavour. She is intelligent, insightful and courageous, and has been a boon in all—"

"And you are wondering if you have fallen in love with her too quickly," Drestan interrupted.

Ghastly frowned. "How could you possibly have known that?"

"I'm no expert when it comes to love, Ghastly, but I have been around enough to recognise it when I see it."

"The problem is that I have only known her for a mere handful of days."

"And you think, perhaps, that there is a required length of time for love to announce its presence? How old are you, Ghastly?"

Ghastly hesitated. He was always forgetting this. "Well, it's 1703 now, and I was born—"

"I'll save you some time – you're a hundred and

twenty-three years old. What have you learned of love in all those years?"

"Very little," said Ghastly. "Only that it continues to surprise."

"Exactly," said Drestan. "There are no rules. There is no minimum amount of time and no maximum amount of time when it comes to love. It will rear its head of its own accord, and it is no less valid if it rears its head sooner rather than later, or later rather than sooner."

"But surely this kind of love is the stuff of Shakespeare's plays? Romeo and Juliet fell in love at first sight and this is scarcely any better."

"I thought you liked Shakespeare's plays?"

"I like the funny ones, not the sad ones."

"Ghastly, my boy!" said Corrival Deuce, slapping Ghastly on the back upon entering the chamber. "It is good to see you! You're looking strong these days; what have you been eating? No, don't tell me, you'll only make me hungry. I apologise for the interruption, but I must talk to Elder Bizarre regarding several matters of utmost importance and, honestly, one matter of amusing irrelevance."

Ghastly smiled. "Of course. It is good to see you again, Corrival. I shall take my leave."

"Before you do," Drestan said, standing to shake Corrival's hand, "keep in mind one thing: you came to me today not to talk about the woman who travelled back in time to save the world, but the woman who stood with her, who was intelligent, insightful and courageous. Your doubts mean nothing. Your heart knows the truth."

Corrival's eyes widened. "You were discussing matters of the heart? I adore matters of the heart! Tell me!"

Ghastly laughed. "Another time, perhaps," he said, and bowed to them both before leaving.

Having advanced his thinking on this not as far as he would have liked, Ghastly shook it from his head as he approached Valkyrie, who was standing in the corridor, staring at the wall.

"Are you well?" he asked.

She looked at him. "I hate your toilets."

"Pardon?"

"Your toilets. The planks in the floor. The chamberpots. I hate them. You know what I hate more? The sponges. Sponges, for God's sake. When is toilet paper invented? How hard is it to invent toilet paper?"

Ghastly didn't know quite how to extricate himself from this conversation, so he found himself diving in. "We have some toilet paper, as you put it, somewhere, I think, but it is not a very efficient way to clean the... parts. Some people use rags, which I have never been comfortable with, but I could recommend some good grasses or seashells, if that is more to your liking."

She frowned at him. "Seashells? How the hell do you...? You know what? It's fine. I'm just gonna be constipated the entire bloody time I'm here. It's grand. No big deal."

"I know of some good-sized leaves..."

"Ghastly, really, you can stop. See, the problem is that I never went camping as a kid. Never had to find a bush in the woods to go behind. I've been spoiled, basically. I've lived my life with the luxury of indoor plumbing. I've been pampered every step of the way."

He hesitated before speaking again. "There are magic toilets."

Valkyrie blinked. "There are?"

"There will be. I have heard rumours that they are working on magic toilets. I do not know how they operate or what would make them different from ordinary latrines, but that is what I have heard."

"Magic toilets," she said softly. "How wonderful."

They started walking back towards the main hall, where Skulduggery was waiting.

"The fact that we are friends in the future," Skulduggery said to Valkyrie as they approached, "presumably means that I am still capable of *having* friends, yes?"

She sat on the bench next to him and Ghastly stood nearby. Everyone else had given her a wide berth, so she was probably feeling quite isolated.

"Very much so," she said, suddenly seeming a lot more at ease. Perhaps being around a younger version of Skulduggery, even though he didn't have the memories of the one she knew, was enough to relax her.

"That is good news," Skulduggery said. "The friends I have now do not seem to trust me very much."

Valkyrie arched an eyebrow. "Can you blame them?"

"Absolutely not," he said. "I don't even trust me, and I *am* me."

Something was bothering Ghastly. "Isn't this dangerous, this conversation? When Sensitives see something dreadful about to happen, it is perfectly normal to try to circumnavigate fate because the future has not happened yet. But you are *from* the future, and so any change you instigate to your own past could very well unravel your entire existence."

"I'm not an expert in this," Valkyrie said, "but my sister, a version of my sister, she travelled in time once and, when her past was altered, she didn't change. Granted, she hasn't returned to her own time, and there's the possibility that if she ever does she'd just stop existing and be replaced by a chronologically correct version of herself – but there's also a theory that time-travellers would be exempt from chronological-correctness."

"A natural immunity," said Skulduggery.

"Exactly. Once this is over, and I return to my own time, I'll either revert to the person I was before I left, with no memory of the last few days here, or I'll stay as I am with the memories I'm currently making."

"Time-travel is complicated."

"Isn't it just?"

Skulduggery ran his hand over his skull as if he still had hair. It was an unconscious movement, an echo of something he used to do back when he was alive, but something he did less and less of now. "What happened to Serpine in your timeline?"

Valkyrie considered her answer before speaking, and then sighed. "He struck a deal when the war ended. There was this amnesty thing and he got to remain free so long as he persuaded others to stop fighting."

Skulduggery tilted his head. "The war was over, Serpine was a free man, and I did not find him and kill him? Why is that, do you know?"

"I don't, sorry."

"There must be a reason."

"I never asked," she said. "You get... quiet when you talk about that part of your life. I never wanted to intrude. Which is very unlike me because I am quite nosy when it comes to stuff like that."

"Oh, I do not think I would agree," said Skulduggery. "Your nose is entirely in proportion with the rest of your face."

Valkyrie smiled. "No, I don't mean, like, I have a large nose. I just mean *nosy*. You know, inquisitive. Curious."

His head tilted again, this time in the other direction.

"That might be a phrasing we do not yet have. Nosy. Huh. Why is being curious called being nosy?"

"I literally have no idea."

"Ah. That is very definitive of you."

"Oh, well, it is, and I don't have any idea at all, whatsoever, but just for the sake of clarity, in the future, we don't always mean *literally* to mean *literally*. Sometimes we use *literally* to mean something that's really not literal at all, in the slightest. It's just a way to emphasise something."

"And yet," Skulduggery responded, "one would imagine that expanding the meaning of literally would actually negate its very meaning."

"Yeah, it totally does."

"The future would seem to be a complicated place."

"Yeah, it totally is." She brightened. "So how's life right now? What's going on in the world?"

"I would like to say that the mortals are doing a fantastic job, but then I would be lying," Skulduggery said. "Let me see, what has been happening? They just passed the Popery Act here, which is a scheme to reduce the land owned by Catholics. Last year, England crowned a new queen, then went to war with France and Spain."

Ghastly nodded. "The year before, a state in America called Massachusetts went without food for a day to say sorry for the wrongful persecution of witches. An entire day!"

"Almost thirty years ago," Skulduggery said, "seventy-one people were executed in Sweden, all in the same day, for practising witchcraft, and not one of them was an actual witch. Sometimes I wonder if maybe we would be better off just taking control. It genuinely would be in the mortals' best interests."

"I know a few sorcerers who've thought the same way over the years," said Valkyrie.

"And what happened to them?"

"You and me have had to go in and sort them out."

He looked at her, and laughed. "That does sound like fun."

Rustica walked up, stuffing tobacco into her pipe with her thumb. She looked around and Ghastly smiled, headed over, clicking his fingers to generate a small flame.

"Ah," his mother said as he lit the pipe, "thank you, sweetheart." She puffed a few times, then glanced at Skulduggery and Valkyrie. "You know who she is," she said softly. "You do because I've told you of her."

Ghastly frowned. "The girl from your vision? But

Valkyrie is older than her, surely. You told me the girl was no more than eighteen years."

"She is older, I grant you," Rustica answered. "Older and stronger, more powerful and infinitely sadder. But she is the same girl I saw in my vision, of this I am certain – the one who will become Skulduggery's companion and die a terrible death."

"Maybe her death was averted," Ghastly said.

"I do not think it was, and yet she lives still." A shrug. "I cannot explain it. Just one more unexplainable thing to add to my list."

Her pipe went out and he clicked his fingers, lighting it for her again.

"How have you been, Mother?"

"I have been how I have been," she said, smiling at him. "I change, as the seasons change, as we all change: every cycle similar but not quite the same as the last. And you, my sweet boy?"

"I have been me, which is enough."

"I see you are still plunging into danger with your friends."

He smiled. "How else is there to greet danger than by plunging into it?"

"There are safer ways to live."

"None that suit me quite yet. I can see a time, though, once this war is over, when I will embrace the quiet and the unexciting, when I will make clothes and raise a family of my own."

Her hands went to her chest. "A family? With grandchildren?"

"And plenty of them."

"And that is all I have ever wanted. The sight fails me sometimes when it comes to you, so I have been kept aloft by hope and hope alone. But grandchildren! Finally!"

Ghastly laughed. "If you so sorely need children running around, you still have a century or two to provide me with brothers and sisters."

She waved that away. "I want the delight of children, not the burden nor the responsibility."

"A burden, was I?"

"Only in the best possible way," she said, eyes twinkling. "But, before we talk about you as a father, first we talk about the mother. Any prospects I should know about?"

"It is not that easy. Like you said, we plunge into

danger, which tends to worry some more delicate prospects, and, even when the Dead Men aren't together, I am off fighting Mevolent's agents all over the world, which puts a strain on any relationship. Plus..." He gestured at his face.

Rustica arched an eyebrow. "Yes?"

Ghastly sighed. "My scars prove to be somewhat off-putting."

"Your scars are beautiful."

"Not everyone agrees."

"Each scar is part of you, and, if you are beautiful, then each scar is beautiful."

"I am ugly, Mother, but that's all right – I am quite used to it."

She looked at him sternly. "You are not ugly."

"Thank you, but you have to say that as my mother. I am not upset at the term, by the way – I am simply resigned to the truth."

She held his hand. "Naturally, I am biased – in that, you are absolutely correct – but beauty is not about how pretty you are, just as ugliness is not about how far you veer from someone else's idea of perfection. Your scars have allowed you to see past other people's flaws. Would you be as decent as you are, as empathetic, as caring, without them? They have made you a better person. They have made you a beautiful person. Look at me. Your father is a skilled healer, and yet is my nose perfectly straight, or has it been noticeably broken and reset countless times? Are my ears delicate, or battered? Does my jaw click when I speak sometimes? I have never asked him to heal all my wounds. I want to wear my experience in my countenance. Every line, every wrinkle, every bruise and scar is a story of who I am and how I came to be. Not all of them are good stories. Some are sad, some are hurtful, some are scary – but they are, all of them, mine. They all make up who I am. And tell me, my lovely, sweet boy, am I beautiful?"

He smiled. "You are the most beautiful in all the land."

"You see? As my son, you had to say that. But that does not mean it isn't true."

The door opened and Tome looked in. "The Elders are ready."

16

The Dead Men assembled in the Great Chamber, Rustica, Valkyrie and Rapture beside them. Meritorious and Crow swept in and took their chairs. Only Drestan Bizarre's remained empty.

"Our original plan still stands," Meritorious said. "The Dead Men and a team from Mevolent's forces will make its way to the Gate to Hell. Using whatever means necessary, they will secure the Gate, and then Mevolent will seal it shut." He paused. "But that still leaves us with Strickent Abhor – a man who should not be here, and whose presence complicates matters to a potentially devastating degree. We simply have no way of knowing the true extent of his powers. We have no way of knowing if he could reopen the Gate with a wave of his hand. In short, he must be dealt with. He must be sent back to his own time.

"The Council of Elders have spoken with our most learned scholars, and we have a possible solution to our problem. This Unix Blade you spoke of, Valkyrie, the knife that has marked the mortal man, Tithonus, throughout his own lifetime – we believe this is key. Because of this knife, Tithonus is the anchor that keeps Abhor here, where he does not belong. Do you know where Abhor keeps it?"

"On his belt," said Valkyrie.

"Good. Our scholars are reasonably certain that the Unix Blade, because of the properties it has been imbued with, would kill Tithonus, and thus send Abhor back to your time."

Valkyrie frowned. "Your plan is to kill an innocent man? That doesn't strike me as exactly fair."

"I doubt whether time-travel is an area in which fair ever gets a decent chance."

"An innocent man," said Skulduggery, "that you want *us* to kill, yes?"

Crow raised an eyebrow the barest of fractions. "If you are unwilling to get this man's blood on your hands, we have plenty of other killers to call upon."

Skulduggery tilted his head. "No. I can do it."

"Excellent."

"We still need to wield the knife," said Ghastly. "It will not be easy getting close to someone with Strickent's power."

"To go after one knife of power," said Meritorious, "you need another knife of power." He took a thin blade from its sheath. "The first cut of *this* knife will pass through stone and metal. It should be enough to at least *hurt* Strickent Abhor, but the first thrust is the only one that matters. Try it a second time, the knife is just a knife. You have to get close enough to use it, and you have to be fast enough to make it count."

He sheathed the knife and held it towards Skulduggery.

"Give it to Hopeless," Skulduggery said. "We cannot afford to make a mistake."

Meritorious nodded, and Hopeless accepted the weapon, slipping it up his sleeve.

The two Elders stood. "Nefarian Serpine will be shackled," Meritorious said, "then handed over to Mevolent in a show of good faith. Skulduggery, can you be trusted to be a part of this, or do you think it best to focus on the mission ahead?"

"If anyone is to hand Serpine back to the enemy," Skulduggery said, "it should be me."

"That is what I thought you would say. I need not remind you that Serpine must remain unharmed while he is in our custody."

Skulduggery nodded. "Serpine must remain relatively unharmed. I understand."

"Completely unharmed, Skulduggery."

"Practically unharmed, you have my word."

Elder Crow sighed. "Sagacious, take Skulduggery to the dungeon to prepare the prisoners for transport. The rest of you, accompany them and make sure Skulduggery doesn't murder anyone."

Tome teleported them to the dungeon. Zeal sat on the bed in her cell, her head down, but Serpine was on his feet.

"Sagacious," he said solemnly, "if the Elders are sending you, that must mean they have arrived at a momentous decision. You are here to bring me to my execution, are you not? Please, be honest with me. My end has come, yes? You are the only one they would trust with something like this. Let me gaze into your dull eyes and – yes! Yes, you are here to kill me! I know it!" He reeled from the bars dramatically.

No one was amused by the display. "Nefarian Serpine," Tome said, "you are to accompany a delegation to a meeting with Mevolent on neutral ground, where you will be released into his custody as a sign of—"

Serpine gasped. "I am to be released? I am to be freed? By what miracle is this? Oh, you jest! You jest, I know you do! You cruel, cruel man! The years you've spent scurrying after this Council of Elders has made you bitter! How could you toy with my—?"

"Would you shut up?" Tome shouted.

Serpine laughed. "So it is true. You are being forced to release me. I have spent one solitary night in shackles and you are being forced to let me go. How does that make you feel, Sagacious? What say you, assorted Dead Men? Does it, perhaps, make you feel inadequate? Ineffectual? Worthless?"

"We caught you once," said Dexter, "we'll do it again."

Serpine smiled at him. "I think not."

Skulduggery approached the cell, taking his time and not saying anything. Shudder and Ravel stayed close to him in case he lunged, managed to grab Serpine through the bars and snap his neck. Ghastly joined them. Just to be sure.

"This must hurt," said Serpine, standing so very still, within easy reach. "It must kill you, all over again, to be this close to your revenge and have it denied to you. You have been hunting me for years. Every step I have taken since the day you came back, I have felt you behind me. I have known you were there, getting closer. I've never been able to settle, never been able to feel secure. And now I stand before you and you can't do one single thing to pay me back for everything I have taken."

"The Hidden God can help you," Zeal said before Skulduggery could respond. She was looking up at him now, her eyes shining with the same electric blue that infected Strickent's.

"Sister," Rapture said with infinite sadness, "once we are finished here, we will get you the help you sorely need. You are lost, my sister, but you need not be alone."

"Lost to the Lady of Darkness?" Zeal responded. "I

most certainly am. You are not my sister, Rapture. You never were. And she is not my Lady."

Rapture shook her head. "Then you are not only lost to us, you are lost to reason. Lost to love."

"You do not know love until the Hidden God changes you. You do not know reason until he whispers in your ear. He has shown me the true way, the way out of the darkness. His power is unfathomable." Zeal fixed her blue eyes on Skulduggery. "He can bring back the ones you have lost."

Serpine laughed. "Yes, skeleton, put your faith in this one's new-found god. She glimpsed his face for a scant moment and has been converted. Praise his name! Of course, if he could truly bring back your wife and child, if he could truly raise the dead, I doubt he would need to cheat his way to recruiting followers by having them hurled through his portal of many colours. What sensible person would not happily fall in line for a chance to see their loved ones again?"

Zeal turned her gaze towards Serpine. "You wish the Hidden God to squander his miracles on the undeserving?"

"I wish him to be anything but the charlatan he so clearly is," Serpine replied. "If you are seeking someone to worship and you have found your precious Lady of Darkness undeserving, why settle for this ridiculous sorcerer on the other side of a portal when the Faceless Ones are ready for your endless devotion and lifetime of servitude?"

"The Faceless Ones are creatures of spite and pettiness," Zeal said. "The Hidden God is the force behind the universe."

"Your Hidden God hides."

"And your Faceless Ones flee."

Serpine grunted, and turned back to Skulduggery. "Is this the torture you have devised for me – a theological debate with an inferior mind? Truly, you are far more sadistic than I ever would have imagined, as this is an argument I clearly cannot win. The stupid never know when they are beaten."

Zeal smiled. "And yet only an inferior mind would confuse simplicity with stupidity."

"Your god cannot bring back the dead," said Serpine, taking one step closer to the bars. "Forget about the quiet ravings of this fanatic and her ridiculous god, Skulduggery. This moment is between us. You have had it play out in your head just as I have had it play out in mine. Do you remember how your family screamed? Do you remember how your child begged you to save them? How your wife cried, knowing what was about to happen? Do you remember that? You make me laugh, you really do. Your impotence, it amuses me. It will amuse me more in the weeks and months and years to come, as I think back to this day. Do you notice how close your fellow Dead Men stand to you? That is because they have been ordered to protect me – to protect me from you. I am standing right in front of you and I have never been safer."

A moment, frozen.

Skulduggery lunged and Ghastly grabbed one arm and Ravel and Shudder grabbed the other and they held him, they held him back, and Serpine laughed with a singular joy, but darkness exploded, bursting through Skulduggery's shirt and his coat, bursting from his eye sockets, tendrils of shadow that tore through Serpine's body with such force they threw him backwards. He didn't fall, though – he couldn't. He was held aloft by those tendrils, held aloft and screaming as they burrowed inside him, wrapping around every part of him, his screams reaching incredible new heights and then, with one terrible convulsion, they took him apart. The tendrils retracted, disappearing within Skulduggery.

Ghastly released him, stepped back. Shudder and Ravel stumbled away, and Skulduggery fell to one knee.

"What," Valkyrie said, "the hell?"

17

The Dead Men waited in the corridor outside the dungeon and Valkyrie paced.

"This is wrong," she said, shaking her head. "This is all so completely wrong. Serpine isn't supposed to die yet, not for hundreds of years. This doesn't make any sense."

Ghastly watched her. "You said it yourself – as a time-traveller, you expected to effect some degree of change."

She spun on her heel towards him. "I came back to

stop Strickent from screwing everything up. But I'm under strict instructions not to let anyone change anything big."

"It is safe to say you have failed," said Ravel.

She scowled. "Yeah, I got that, thanks."

Ravel frowned. "You are thanking me, but I do not think you mean it."

"Oh, God," said Valkyrie, resuming pacing, "please tell me sarcasm has been invented by now."

"Sarcasm exists," Ghastly told her, "but you might use it in a different context than we do."

"So you guys do old-fashioned sarcasm? Well, that's just brilliant, that is."

Ravel's frown deepened. "Is she doing it again? I really cannot tell."

"I have a question," Saracen said. "You hold the memory of Serpine dying at some stage in the future, yes? You witnessed this?"

"I did," said Valkyrie.

"And yet he has just died here, hundreds of years before that death, which means he cannot die a second time, so you cannot witness it. If we are all agreed on the simple logic of what I have just said, why do you still remember how he died? Would not the memory be immediately wiped from your mind?"

"I mean, yeah," said Valkyrie, "if we were just dealing with time-travel, the memory would probably be replaced with something else. But something happened in my time, quite recently, and reality got rewritten, in a way. Some changes were made that we're still trying to catalogue. If reality is still capable of being rewritten, then maybe I'm able to remember both timelines in the same way I was allowed to remember both versions of reality. Which means even though I recall things the way they originally unfolded, in the new timeline Serpine is already dead by the time I'm even born, so he doesn't kill my uncle, and I might not ever find out about magic. But then what does that actually mean? When I go back to my own time, will I still be me? Is there another me who never found out about magic and will I turn into her? How much of me will I lose?"

"You talk about your timeline being the original timeline," Shudder said, "and this timeline being the aberration – yet, by your own admission, is not your original timeline itself a second timeline?"

"I... think so?" said Valkyrie. "Probably? Yeah, I guess

it would be. It's complicated, though, so I don't want to say too much. Oh, God, I hate this. I literally hate this so much."

Ghastly frowned. "When you said literally just there—"

"I literally mean literally."

"And when you said literally just *there*—"

"Ghastly," Valkyrie said, "now is not the time."

"Of course. Apologies."

"What about the Hidden God?"

"What about him?"

"When Zeal said that he could bring people back from the dead, do you think she was messing?"

"Messing?"

"Messing," said Valkyrie. "Kidding. Joking. Was she lying?"

"Oh. I assume so."

Ravel nodded. "It sounded like a lie."

Dexter shrugged. "This kind of thing is promised all the time. It would be foolhardy to believe anything she says."

"I know that," Valkyrie said. "I know we can't trust her, I know she's probably not telling the truth, and I know the Hidden God probably can't bring back the dead. But what if we're wrong? I've screwed up the timeline. I've failed to stop the future, *your* future, from being changed. So I have to fix it."

"What you are suggesting goes against the natural order," said Shudder.

"The natural order has already been gone against, dude."

"Valkyrie," Rapture said, "out of all the people in the world who have died unjust deaths, you want to bring Nefarian Serpine back to life?"

"I have to," Valkyrie said, her pacing becoming frenetic. "In order for me to get to this point, in order for this conversation to actually happen, Serpine has to kill my uncle. It's how the timeline unfolds. It's how..."

Words failed her and she broke from her pacing pattern and stormed off. They watched her go, and nobody said anything for a while.

"Interesting, is it not?" Dexter murmured eventually. "For her, every step we take is the wrong one, ushering us towards destinies that have been rewritten. How awful it must be, how terrifying, to watch the world divert from its course."

"But for us," said Saracen, "life continues ever onwards. What do we know of our destinies? How can we judge the distance we have strayed? And why should we care? Surely one destiny is as valid as any other."

Ravel frowned at them both. "This is unlike you."

"In what way?" asked Saracen.

Ravel glanced at Shudder and then at Hopeless, and when neither of them leaped in to help, he looked at Ghastly.

Ghastly searched for a nice way to say it. "Usually, neither of you think quite so much."

"Ah," said Dexter, folding his arms and leaning against the wall, "but, when dealing with questions such as those we are dealing with, what choice do we have but to ponder the possibilities?"

"We can think interesting thoughts if the situation calls for interesting thoughts to be thought," said Saracen. "It is hardly our fault if the situations until now have failed to challenge us, intellectually."

"And what conclusion, if any, have you reached?" asked Shudder.

"The conclusion," Dexter responded, "is that there is

no conclusion, as a conclusion indicates the existence of a correct answer or a right choice. But here there is neither. In the past, an event would occur – good, bad, or indifferent – and the response of any one of us would be to shrug and say *so be it*."

Saracen narrowed his eyes. "But can we say *so be it* now? Is there even an *it* to *be*? For there to be an *it* to *be*, there would have to be a destiny to reach, yes?"

Hopeless frowned. "What?"

"What Saracen is saying," said Dexter, "is that there is no longer a correct course of action. So, if there is no *it* to *be*, then that allows us to break from an invisible structure we never even knew was there. We are free."

"Free from the *it*," said Saracen. "So where does that leave us?"

"I have no idea," confessed Shudder.

Saracen gestured. "Take Ghastly as an example. Look at you. Who are you? What are you? You are a man. A man called Ghastly. Your destiny was what your destiny was. But now it is different. Now we do not know what it was, and so we do not know what it is. You had a destiny, but now that destiny has been replaced."

"Does it matter?" Ghastly asked. "I did not know the first destiny, and I don't know the second, so what has changed?"

"Your freedom to make what you will of your own future," said Dexter. "That has changed. That is different."

Ghastly regarded them. "Perhaps allowing you the chance to think so much was a mistake."

"You are fumbling around for a point, I take it?" Hopeless asked.

"This is Ghastly Bespoke," said Saracen. "A man. A mage. Our friend. Because of recent events, Ghastly is now on a course through his own life that has never existed before. Where will it take him, I wonder?"

"Straight to Sister Rapture," said Dexter.

Ghastly sighed. "Is that what this is about?"

"You think we jest, but we do not. You think we poke fun, but we do not. We are merely suggesting that recent events have cast you into each other's celestial orbit where, before, they did not."

Ghastly watched them and said nothing.

"The opportunity that lies before you has never existed

before now," Saracen said. "Surely you are obliged to seize it, if only to spite capricious fate and all of its cruelties?"

"All of its many cruelties," said Dexter.

"Each of us has lost loves and seen friends die. Each of us has watched people we adore get caught in the machinery of time and circumstance, be pulled into the gears, twisted and snapped by events beyond our control. That is what fate does to us. But now it is vulnerable. The machine is not working like it should, and so we can reach in, change it, form something new."

"Interesting," said Ravel.

"Potentially interesting," said Hopeless.

Shudder said nothing.

"Perhaps," said Ghastly, somewhat reluctantly. "Perhaps you are right. Perhaps I should seize the opportunity. But, if I should, then shouldn't you? If we all have been gifted with the chance to do something we would not ordinarily do, then what are you going to do? What change would you make?"

Saracen and Dexter looked at each other, but said nothing.

"Ghastly," Sagacious Tome said, walking over, "Meritorious would like a word."

His wrists shackled, Skulduggery didn't look up when Ghastly walked in. The room was in a dark and quiet and cold level of the Sanctuary. It was small and lit by candles. Ghastly sat down at the table Skulduggery was resting his elbows on.

"How do you feel?" he asked.

Skulduggery didn't answer for a long moment.

"Cheated," he said at last.

"You are the one who killed him. You got your revenge."

"My revenge was never about killing him. My revenge was in everything leading up to that point."

Ghastly peeled a long splinter off the edge of the table. "So you wield dual disciplines – you are an Elemental and a Necromancer."

"I am not a Necromancer."

"You may not have studied it, you may not belong to the Order or worship at the Temple, but that was death-magic you used to kill Serpine."

Skulduggery raised his head, finally looking at Ghastly.

"Fitting, I suppose, as Necromancy was what he used to kill me. But I did not mean to do it. I wanted to kill him in that moment, yes – I wanted to choke the life out of him – but I did not want to kill him like that."

"How long have you known you could do this?"

"I experimented when I was young, before I chose to be an Elemental."

"You never told me."

"This is a group of people who revere death above all else – I was only going to tell you if I had decided to join them. But the more Necromancers I spoke to, the less appealing it became. It was Morwenna Crow, actually, who talked me out of pursuing it any further."

"Why did she do that?" Ghastly asked.

"She said I was unsuitable. She said I liked the power too much, and someone like me would do terrible things with it. I believed her, and walked away."

"And that was the end of it? You did not indulge your Necromancer side any further?"

Skulduggery didn't respond.

"Ah," said Ghastly.

"It has been useful. I practised just enough to keep the option open to me. My brothers and sisters, they all wield two disciplines – one that they are happy to demonstrate to others, and one that they keep secret."

"I know some of your family quite well, and I did not know that."

"My siblings are good at keeping secret things secret."

"So you thought it would be easy," said Ghastly, "maintaining your affinity for Necromancy? Keeping it for special occasions, as it were?"

"I saw no reason why it would not be."

"And then, just a few hours ago..."

"I do not know what happened. I have never lost control like that."

"You killed a prisoner in our custody."

"I am aware."

"So you are also aware of what the punishment is for such a crime."

"I am."

Ghastly put the key to the shackles down on the table. "Meritorious is hoping to avoid that, if at all possible."

Skulduggery paused. "He intends to spare me?"

"What did Shakespeare say?" asked Ghastly. "*He must needs go that the devil drives.*"

"Lydgate said it first."

"Obviously, Lydgate said it first, I am not claiming otherwise, all I am doing is... Dear God, you are just making this awkward, are you not? Listen to me, you fool. When we fail to hand Serpine over to Mevolent, there is a very good chance that he will withdraw his support for this joint mission of ours. If that happens, we will have to be ready to go in ourselves. Saracen and I will accompany the delegation to the meeting; you will lead the others into San Gimignano."

"We shall take Sister Zeal with us," Skulduggery said. "She might be able to get us closer to Strickent."

"Taking her increases our risk," Ghastly said, and sighed. "Very well. If I fail to join you before midnight, assume something has gone dreadfully wrong, and get to the Gate. You need to clear it and hold it, and if you can grab the Unix Blade while you are there, so much the better."

"Strickent will be waiting for us," said Skulduggery.

Ghastly nodded. "This is not the first time the Dead Men have walked into a conflict we cannot win, but it may very well be the last."

"So Meritorious is willing to spare my life *now* just so I can die later," Skulduggery said, picking up the key. "That sounds eminently reasonable."

"I thought you might like it."

Skulduggery unlocked his shackles and they stood.

"If all this goes according to plan, however," said Ghastly, "and you survive, you will probably have to live the rest of your life in exile."

"Seeing as how all of my friends will probably be dead by that stage, I have no problem with that."

18

By nightfall, they'd moved a grand table into the tent outside San Gimignano, and placed two chairs on either side. The place was lit with candles and covered lanterns. Sanctuary banners hung heavily by the south entrance, and by the north some banners for Mevolent's forces had been draped – black banners, slashed with red.

Meritorious sat in one of the chairs. Crow sat beside him. Ghastly stood at Meritorious's right hand, Saracen at Crow's left. Tome stood nearby with Rustica, Bliss, and the silent, eerily still Cleavers. Their army –

invisible to mortals – was camped less than half a league behind them, the rest of the Dead Men were already in San Gimignano, and the two chairs on the other side of the table were empty. Mevolent was keeping them waiting.

"This is ridiculous," Elder Crow muttered.

"Let him play his games," said Meritorious.

"There is no more time for games. Did we not stress enough the need for urgency? I thought we had. I thought we had made that quite clear."

"For some people, Morwenna, a game is only a game if they are the ones having all the fun."

Saracen squared his shoulders. "They are here," he announced. "Meritorious, Vengeous, the Voice, the Teleporter we met that time in Belgium."

"Peregrine," said Ghastly.

"That's the one. They've got Brobding with them, and four others."

"One of whom is a Sensitive," said Rustica. "He's stopping me from getting an impression of mood."

"As we expected," Meritorious murmured.

The Voice scurried in first, sneering at the Elders like this was all part of some grand jape. He bowed theatrically.

"Grand Mage Meritorious, Elder Crow, esteemed warriors and wise counsels, I bid you greetings from Mevolent, the Lord of Sorcerers and the Master of the World, may all the unworthy fall before his might. My Lord offers the sincerest of apologies for keeping you waiting as if you were little more than witless servants. He hopes this did not wound your delicate pride, as Sanctuary mages are known to be fragile creatures, prone to taking offence at the slightest of slights. If any of you wish to weep, wail, or caterwaul, he offers you a moment to do so with as much dignity as you can scrape together, before he enters."

Meritorious sighed. "We shall struggle on, thank you."

The Voice bit his lower lip. "So brave. I am humbled to be in your presence."

"Get on with it, toad," said Crow.

The Voice simpered. The tent flaps swept aside and the enemy contingent walked in, Brobding having to stoop to fit. The air rippled slightly and Mevolent's chair slid out, settling behind him as he sat. Vengeous took the other chair. His pack of killers stood ready.

"The Lord of Sorcerers and Master of the World

cannot help but notice that you do not have Nefarian Serpine with you," said the Voice.

Meritorious kept his eyes on Mevolent. "We have decided to hold on to Serpine for the time being – to ensure your co-operation."

The Voice sniffed haughtily. "The Master's word is his bond."

"And we have not had your word. When we get through this, providing you can keep from double-crossing us, your general will be returned to you."

Mevolent observed him, and the Voice didn't say anything.

"Where are the rest of the Dead Men?" Vengeous asked. He was clad in heavy leather and light armour, and looked eager for battle.

"They are close by," Crow said. "Sagacious Tome will be accompanying you on your mission, as will two Masked Sisters."

"The nuns can come, but Tome stays here. We have our own Teleporter, one who has already visited every corner of that squalid little town."

Crow laughed. "If you think we are going to trust your man to teleport our people out of danger, I would hazard that you have taken one too many blows to the head, Baron."

"Our Teleporter is better suited to the task, Elder Crow. Unless you have some reason to insist on Mr Tome, such as a plot to betray this temporary alliance of ours, Mr Peregrine would seem to be the logical choice."

"Very well," said Meritorious. "But are you taking the giant with you?"

Brobding tried to draw himself up to his full height, but his head brushed the tent's ceiling and he scowled and stayed stooped.

"We might be in need of pure physical strength," Vengeous said.

"He is too big. Too easily spotted. Mr Bliss can take his place."

Vengeous glared at Bliss, who looked back at him with remarkable indifference. "Bliss is a treacherous heathen who went against his own family, and we do not trust him."

"Mr Bliss has always known his own mind, despite the pressures of family, and, if you do feel the need for pure physical strength, I daresay you would leap at the chance to have him on your side. Unless there is some reason why you would not want him – such as a plot to betray this temporary alliance of ours."

Vengeous didn't answer.

"Mr Bliss is welcome to join the mission," the Voice said. "Brobding, you shall remain here."

Brobding nodded, failing to contain a smile, and Ghastly frowned. He glanced over at his mother, who had a pained scowl on her face and three fingers pressed into her forehead just over her left eye. Standing beside her, Tome hadn't noticed.

"The Lord of Sorcerers and Master of the World believes that the time has come to go over your plans for tonight's action," said the Voice. "He is prepared to take command of the operation once your deficiencies became apparent. Oh, sorry – I mean *if* your deficiencies become apparent, of course."

Tome finally noticed Rustica's discomfort, and he leaned in, whispering. Upon her answer, he immediately stepped towards the table, eyes on the enemy. In that instant, Ghastly put a hand on Meritorious's shoulder, but a beam of energy, so intense he could feel the heat through his clothes, sliced through the tent wall behind

Mevolent and took apart the Grand Mage's head before he had a chance to move. Mevolent flipped the table with one hand and one of his killers came for Ghastly with a blade in his hand. Ghastly left his axe in his belt and bashed the knife-thrust to one side, reducing the killer's jaw to a loosely connected string of broken bones with two blows from his fists.

The table settled over the body of Eachan Meritorious, and Vengeous dived over it at Saracen as Bliss collided with Brobding. Rustica charged and the Cleavers leaped, scythes flashing. Peregrine vanished and came back with more of Mevolent's soldiers armed with swords and axes and crossbows.

A quarrel struck Crow in the shoulder and her shadows, which had pierced the chests of the three men who had rushed her, turned to nothing but smoke. She fell back and Tome caught her. A woman with fire in her hands lunged at them and Tome had to drop the Elder in order to throw himself at their attacker.

Rustica plunged her knife into the throat of a man yelling a war cry. Bliss reduced Brobding's skull to mere kindling and Ghastly's axe bit into the neck of one of the soldiers protecting Mevolent. The Voice squealed and scuttled away and Ghastly used the air to hurl himself forward. Mevolent dodged his axe without much effort.

Ghastly swung again and again, and Mevolent caught his wrist and almost broke it in his grip. Then Bliss was upon him and they went down, rolling across the floor, tangled in the legs of killers, and Ghastly was sent stumbling. He righted himself and brought the axe up and this time it found its target, thudding heavily beneath some ribs. Ghastly pulled it free and grabbed whoever was closest, introducing a large man's nose to his scarred forehead with much enthusiasm.

A sword cut through his leg and Ghastly hissed and buried his axe in a shoulder. A stream of energy sizzled into his side, but it didn't have the focus of the stream that had killed Meritorious, so it scorched his flesh, but failed to put him down. A crossbow quarrel whispered by his ear. He was aware that he was shouting, but his shouts were lost behind the sounds of the fighting. He doubted he was making much sense anyway.

Someone crashed into him and they sprawled over the upturned table. He glimpsed his mother jumping in to help Saracen against Vengeous. Crow lay dead on the floor, a knife in her chest. Tome reeled by, bleeding from a long gash in his face. The Cleavers fell under swords and axes and streams of energy. Mr Bliss flew backwards, hit the upper corner of the tent and that whole side started to collapse.

Ghastly looked up to see Mevolent step towards him. Rustica gripped Saracen, and Tome grabbed her hand and then grabbed Ghastly's, and before Ghastly had taken his next breath they were all under the night sky, thick with dark and heavy clouds, on the hill overlooking Meritorious's army. Mevolent's forces were sweeping through the camp, lit by burning tents, as soldiers Ghastly had stood beside ran for weapons and tried to fight back. The sounds of the slaughter mingled with the screams of the dying.

"The mission," Rustica said to Tome, stepping away and unsheathing her sword. "Take these into San Gimignano."

"Mother, no," said Ghastly, scrambling to his feet.

"Strickent Abhor must be stopped and the Gate to Hell must be closed," she said, as much steel in her eyes now as there was in her fist. "Do not let me down, my lovely son. Do not fail in your mission." And then she was running down the hill, towards the fighting.

Ghastly made to go after her, but Saracen stood in his way. He didn't have to say anything. The night roared and Ghastly turned to Tome.

"Hurry."

19

Tome teleported them into San Gimignano, across the street from a tavern with a red door. A mortal saw them arrive and he yelped, staggered back, and ran. They let him go and the red door opened, and Ravel beckoned them inside. The tavern was dark and quiet and empty, save for the Dead Men, Rapture, Valkyrie and Zeal, who was shackled to a heavy support beam.

"They're dead," said Tome, collapsing into a chair, blood dripping from the wound on his face. "Meritorious and Crow are dead."

Saracen looked up from the map on the table. "What?"

"Maybe Bliss, too. I didn't check on him. I should go back. I should check on him."

"No," said Hopeless. "If he is alive, he will make his own way back to our army. If he is dead, you will have endangered yourself for nothing."

"There is no army," Ghastly said. "Mevolent's soldiers had somehow got inside the camp before the attack began. We didn't stand a chance."

In the tavern, the silence stretched.

"There will be time for retribution later," said Shudder, hefting a longaxe.

"Your mother," Rapture said to Ghastly. "Is she all right?"

He pulled his hood up over his scars. "The last I saw of Rustica Strife, she was running towards the fighting. As is her way."

"Soon, we will join her," said Skulduggery. "First we deal with the issue in front of us, then we avenge the fallen."

"How do we proceed?" Rapture asked. "Mevolent is the only one who could seal the Gate."

"Then our mission has changed," Skulduggery said.

"Sealing the Gate is no longer an option. We are going to kill Tithonus."

"Seriously?" said Valkyrie. Her braids had come loose so she'd taken them out, and now Ghastly watched as she tied her hair back from her face. "The worst part of the old plan is the only part of the new plan?"

"Nobody needs to die," Zeal said from where she stood. "I will take you to the Hidden God in peace and you will feel his love grow within you, like I did."

"Will you please shut up?" Valkyrie snapped, and Shudder went over and fastened a gag over Zeal's mouth. Valkyrie turned to Skulduggery. "Why? Why should we kill the only truly innocent person in all this?"

"Because I suspect that the Elders only told us half of what needs to be done," he answered. "They wanted us to use the Unix Blade to kill Tithonus in this time period. They would have then given the knife to you, Valkyrie, and allowed you to return to the future – at which stage your own experts would have told you what needed to be done."

"Which would be?"

"As we know, Tithonus cannot die by conventional means and methods. Meritorious told us, however, that the Unix Blade would be capable of such an impossible feat."

"But you're saying the Unix Blade isn't capable of doing it?"

"No, I am merely suggesting that killing Tithonus *once* with the knife would not be enough. I propose using it to kill him in two different time periods – first in the present, and then again in the future. This, I believe with reasonable certainty, would result in a successful death."

"See, at first I was confused, and now I'm just bewildered. How can he be killed in my time if he's already dead in yours?"

"He will not be," said Skulduggery. "I strongly suspect that killing him for the first time will merely prime him for death. Killing him the second time will ensure it."

"So when he's killed the first time," Valkyrie said, "will he actually die?"

"So long as he is killed the second time, absolutely."

"And if he isn't killed the second time?"

Skulduggery hesitated. "I am not an expert in this, but – seeing as how nobody is – I feel confident that there would be the possibility of the very notion of time being torn asunder and that the universe would fracture.

So it is very important that he is killed the second time."

"And this course of action will kill Tithonus," said Ghastly, sticking his axe in his belt and picking up a crossbow, "and untether Strickent from our present?"

"Not only that," Skulduggery responded, "but it will close the Gate to Hell in the process. Would you like me to explain the ways in which it would accomplish this and how I came to this conclusion?"

"No," everybody said at once.

Skulduggery nodded. "Then take my word for it: this is how we save the world. Sagacious, you should return now to the Sanctuary."

"No," Tome said, his hand gripping the hilt of his sword. "I am helping you."

"You are too valuable," Skulduggery told him. "If our army's losses are as catastrophic as you say, we are going to need every Teleporter we have to get the injured to safety."

"You are not in charge, damn you!"

"I know," Skulduggery said gently, "and I know you want to fight, but lives depend on you, my friend."

The anger drained from Tome's blood-splattered face, and he nodded, defeated, and vanished.

"Valkyrie," said Skulduggery, "you mentioned earlier that you can see auras – does this mean you can track them, like you would an animal through a forest?"

"Are you asking me if I can find Tithonus? Probably, yeah. I can see some auras through walls, so locating him shouldn't be too much of a problem. He'll be in the poor part of town. That's where he grew up."

"Then we shall move north until you can detect his aura, at which point we will be following you. Once we have the immortal mortal, we double-back to *La Porta dell'Inferno*, dispatching any and all enemies with ease, and proceed onwards to save the day."

"That does sound easy," said Saracen. "I certainly cannot see how a plan like this could possibly fail."

Skulduggery put on his coat, raising the hood over his head. "I admire your confidence, my friend, and I share it. Absolutely nothing could possibly go wrong with any of this so long as everyone remembers our motto: strike from the shadows..."

"Disappear into darkness," the Dead Men finished.

Skulduggery nodded. "Excellent."

*

The streets were mostly empty. There was the occasional voice to be heard as they passed a window, or the tortured whine of two angry cats meeting somewhere in the dark, all set against the raucous song of the cicadas that filled the night air. What the Dead Men couldn't hear was the sound of battle. They couldn't hear the men and women fighting for their lives just half a league away. The shouts and screams of the dying and the desperate, of the defeated and their killers, travelled no further than the outer reaches of the interlocking bubbles of the cloaking spheres.

They moved on and heard, from round the next corner, laughter – and an animal yelping.

They peered round the edge of the building. Three men, converts to the Hidden God judging by the delight they took in experimenting with their new powers on a cornered dog that bounced and whirled in fear and pain. Beyond them, a man and a woman stood facing away, and a little further on, a crowd. All within shouting distance of one another.

It was too risky to do anything to put a stop to this. Far too risky.

"Hopeless," Skulduggery whispered. "Put a stop to it."

Hopeless nocked an arrow, took a single step out as he drew the string taut, and let fly. He was stepping back even as the arrow hit one of the converts, lodging in the side of his neck. The man gagged and stumbled backwards and fell. The others were too caught up in their animal torture to notice.

Hopeless nocked a second arrow, took another step out from behind the corner, and put this one through the head of the tallest convert. He fell immediately, without a sound, and the remaining convert peered down at him, clearly not comprehending what had just happened. By the time he looked up, Hopeless was releasing a third arrow, and this found its new home deep within the convert's heart.

The dog bolted, losing itself in the twisting labyrinth of the town, and the Dead Men moved on.

The streets grew narrower and the houses grew smaller, and still Valkyrie led them forward, Saracen by her side. At a corner, they crouched and peered round. Ghastly and Rapture hurried up.

Ahead, a boy and girl played hopscotch on an open patch of dirt road, using the moonlight to make out the squares they'd scraped into the ground. The boy was, maybe, ten, the girl perhaps a couple of years older. They were barefoot, their clothes little more than rags.

"That is our only way through," Saracen said softly. "The avenues on either side have too many people. Any one of them could be a convert. Every single one of them could be converts for all we know. We have to pass these children."

"They could just be an ordinary girl and boy," said Ghastly.

Rapture raised an eyebrow. "Playing hopscotch past midnight?"

"It may be a cultural thing," Valkyrie murmured. "Didn't I read somewhere that, historically, Italian kids played hopscotch past midnight, or am I making that up? I might be making it up. I think I am. Oh, man. If they're not ordinary kids, you realise we'll have to fight them, right?"

Rapture shrugged. "Have you ever fought a child? I have not. I would imagine it is quite easy."

"I'm not worried about losing to a kid – I'm worried about hitting one."

"Oh," said Rapture. "Yes. That would be awful."

"You're not a kid person, are you?"

"I never saw the point of them," Rapture said, then plastered on a smile and walked forward. Valkyrie hesitated and did likewise, and the children stopped playing and watched them approach. Ghastly and Saracen stayed where they were.

"*Ciao*," Rapture said, her next words lost to Ghastly, swallowed by the song of the cicadas.

The girl answered, and the boy watched them warily, and Valkyrie nodded along with what was being said.

"Does Valkyrie speak Italian?" Ghastly asked Saracen.

"By the looks of it," Saracen answered, "she does not. I doubt that occurred to her when she stepped forward, however."

Rapture responded to whatever the little girl had said, and laughed, and Valkyrie laughed as well – a little too enthusiastically. She turned the laugh into a cough, and looked up at the clouds like she'd just noticed they threatened rain, but the boy was staring at her now, suspicion darkening his features.

The conversation between Rapture and the little girl dried up, and the little girl frowned.

The boy flung himself at Rapture and the girl opened her mouth wide and vomited a stream of energy that

Valkyrie barely managed to dodge. The girl turned her head, following Valkyrie as she scrambled. The last upchuck of energy caught Valkyrie's leg – would have seared through it were it not for that astonishing suit – and spun her like a top. She hit the ground and the girl took a deep breath, preparing for another heave.

Ghastly ran up, preparing to push at the air, but Valkyrie extended her forefinger and fired a single, thin bolt of lightning that struck the girl in the chest. Howling, the girl reeled away, hands rubbing the point of pain, as Rapture held the little boy's glowing hands away from her.

"*Smettila,*" she said. "*Ti sto avvertendo.*"

The little boy yelled his rage and the little girl came at Valkyrie, who stopped her with a palm to the sternum. She punched the girl lightly on the shoulder, and then the muscle in her thigh. The girl dropped back, clutching her arm and dragging her leg, too overcome with pain to even attempt to use magic.

Valkyrie grabbed the girl by the shoulders and looked to Ghastly. "What's Italian for *go home?*"

"*Andare a casa,*" Ghastly responded.

"*Andare a casa,*" Valkyrie snarled in the girl's face.

"*Tutti lodano il Dio Nacosto!*" the girl screeched. "*Cadi e muori, vecchia!*"

Valkyrie shook her like a rag doll. "I have no idea what you just said," she told her, then flung the girl towards the boy as Rapture flung him towards her. They crashed into each other and fell in a tangled heap and started to cry.

"I feel so incredibly bad right now," Valkyrie said.

"Oh, Valkyrie," said Rapture, "are all people in the future as delicate as you? What age were you when you first fought a grown adult? Seven? Eight?"

"I was twelve."

"And do you think the grown adult that you fought had any qualms about inflicting damage on twelve-year-old you? No? Then why should you have any qualms about inflicting damage on these children? Do you see my point?"

"No, Rapture, not even remotely."

"My point is, children are stupid, and we should carry on."

Skulduggery and the rest of the Dead Men joined them and they hurried away from the wailing children. A few minutes later, they arrived at a shack lodged between two slightly-more-respectable homes. The sound of voices behind them meant they didn't have time to knock, so Valkyrie put her shoulder to the door and it sprang open with a crack of old wood. Rapture and the Dead Men followed her in and Ravel shut the door after them.

The room was lit by a single flickering candle, and the old man sat in the corner, a guitar in his hands. He blinked at them as they neared. He was small and shrunken and incredibly old, with sparse white hair and a long white beard that was little more than tufts of cloud.

"Tithonus," said Valkyrie. "We've come to ask for your help."

"You speak English," Tithonus said. "I try speak English sometimes. Not many people here speak it. Hard to practise if no one speak it. Sometimes I talk to wall in English, to keep the, uh, the habit. But it no very good. Wall is Italian. Wall only speak Italian." Tithonus cackled out a laugh.

"My name is Valkyrie. These are my friends."

"Hello, Valkyrie. Hello, Valkyrie's friends. My name..." He laughed again. "You know my name. You said my name. I had another name once. Not Tithonus." He frowned. "But I remember not what it was." He shrugged. "Why you need help from me? I old man, and weak and stupid, and bad at everything."

Valkyrie sat. "I know about you."

"Yes?"

"I know you're a hundred and forty-two years old."

"Ah," he said. "Magic, yes? Sorcerers?"

"We're sorcerers, yes. I know something else about you, too. I know you're miserable here."

"Very miserable, thank you, yes."

"Tithonus, I'm from the future."

"How nice."

"This is not my first time in San Gimignano. I've been here before, in the twenty-first century. I've spoken to you here."

His saggy face sagged further. "I am alive in this time? Oh, no. This no good. This very no good. Look. Old man. Old man and bad at everything. Hate everything. Can do nothing."

"You can play the guitar," Ghastly said.

"I hold guitar, and remember music. I no play guitar, not in forty years. Fingers, you see? Too old to bend properly." He held up one curled, arthritic hand. "What old man do to help?"

"We want to close the Gate to Hell," said Skulduggery.

"Good!" Tithonus barked, clapping the heel of his hand against the guitar. "Good, yes! But hard to do. Very hard." He peered at him. "*Hai un teschio per testa?*"

"*Sì*," said Skulduggery, pushing down his hood. "*In effetti, sono tutto ossa.*"

Tithonus laughed and clapped his hand against the guitar again. "*Meraviglioso! Un scheletro che vive!*"

"We need you, Tithonus," Skulduggery said. "There is a bad man. A very bad man, and he will hurt many people. He is from the future, like Valkyrie. He is changing history. He must be stopped."

Tithonus nodded, waiting for them to get to the point.

Valkyrie took a breath and let it out. "Tithonus, to stop him and save everyone, we need to kill you."

He laughed. "Old man no die! Old man cannot die! I have tried! I hurt and get older and older, but nothing can kill me! The song of the cicadas – that is my song, yes?"

"We have something that *will* kill you."

His laugh faded. "What is this?"

"A knife. A special knife. A magic knife. We can use it to kill you and... and that's it. Everyone will be saved and you... you'll be dead."

"Magic knife?"

"I'm so sorry, but we need—"

"The magic knife will kill me?"

"Yes. We think so. Yes."

A wide, pretty toothless smile spread. "Oh. Oh, yes. Oh, yes. *Sì*. Now? Go now?"

"Well, I mean... yeah. Do you have anyone to say goodbye to?" Valkyrie asked. "Family, friends, loved ones?"

"Nobody!" Tithonus cackled. "I am old man, and everyone I know is long dead and waiting for me! Let us go! Escort me to my death!"

She shook her head slowly. "I don't know about the rest of you, but this is entirely too grim for my liking."

"Come now, Valkyrie," Skulduggery said, picking up his sword, "we are the Dead Men. Grim is what we do."

20

Dexter by his side, Saracen guided them towards the Gate to Hell while thunder rumbled in the darkness above. Shudder and Zeal stuck close behind, Zeal moving when she was told to move and stopping when she was told to stop. So far, there had been no sign of her trying to break free or raise the alarm, though Ghastly knew Shudder would be growing more alert to any such attempt with every step they took.

Behind Ghastly came Ravel, escorting Tithonus, and

behind Ravel was Rapture, with Valkyrie coming last. Skulduggery and Hopeless were close by – Skulduggery somewhere to the left of them, Hopeless somewhere to the right – little more than ghosts, stealing through the shadows, dispatching any errant enemies before they even knew what was happening.

A single drop of rain fell on Ghastly's scalp, but the skies weren't ready to open quite yet. It was coming, though. The warm air was pressing down upon the streets with a weight he could feel on his skin. The storm was getting ready to break.

"Are you all right?" Rapture asked softly, suddenly at his elbow. "You seem tense."

"I'm fine," he lied.

She nodded, and glanced back at Ravel and Tithonus. While she did so, he looked at her, examining her profile, the slope of her nose, the set of her jaw. There was a notch missing from her left ear, he saw that now, just a tiny piece of cartilage that had long since been sliced away. He returned his attention to their surroundings a moment before she looked back at him.

"I feel as though I have done something wrong," she said.

"No," he responded far too quickly, far too inelegantly. "No, you have done nothing."

"Have I insulted you?"

"Not in the slightest."

"Angered you?"

"I am not angry."

"Then why have you been avoiding me? You have not spoken to me since this morning."

He could either lie and possibly squirm free, or tell the truth and make things worse. He opened his mouth and wondered what words would come out of it.

"I am sorry, but I love you," he said, and winced.

Rapture stopped walking so suddenly it was as if she had sprouted roots from her feet, and he had to take her by the elbow to keep her moving.

"And this is not a joke?" she asked.

"It is not," he said.

"You love me?"

"Yes."

"Yet you have known me a matter of days."

He nodded. "I realise how ridiculous it is."

"How can you love me if you barely know me?"

"In my defence, apart from finding you wonderful and

interesting and intelligent and caring, which are all qualities that, I believe, would make anyone love you, there is also something else at play: a feeling I cannot describe."

"And it is this feeling you blame?"

"Exactly."

"But this feeling is not some alien thing, is it? It is not some external object that you have no influence over. This is a feeling you have generated, that you are responsible for."

"I suppose."

"Then you... you actually love me."

"I actually do."

She frowned. "Why did you apologise?"

"Oh," said Ghastly, his smile broadening before he could stop it, "that was merely a pre-emptive apology."

They got to the next corner, peered round, and hurried into the next patch of darkness.

"And would you typically preface a declaration of love with an anticipatory apology?" Rapture asked, keeping pace.

"I do not typically declare my love, but, on the few occasions when I have, it has been necessary to follow it with an apology, yes."

"For the love of the Lady, why?"

In much the same manner with which he had gestured to his face for his mother, he once again gestured to his face. Rapture opened her mouth and narrowed her eyes, a sure sign he was about to be admonished, but he held up a hand and she bit back her words as Saracen slowed ahead of them.

An old man had wandered into their path. The others caught up, and together they broke from the darkness. The old man saw them and yawned. He had no weapon to reach for and, as they approached, Ghastly recognised him as the man who spent his mornings resting against the well in the *Piazza della Cisterna*. The old man watched, nodding to Saracen and then to the others, and they were almost past him when his eyes lit up. Ghastly filled his hand with fire, but Skulduggery was already stepping from the darkness, his sword taking the man's head even as twin streams of energy burst from those eyes. The body crumpled and the head bounced, the twin streams carving through the air until they sputtered out and died.

"I have seen him before," Ghastly said. "He is from here. I do not think he was even a sorcerer."

Skulduggery let his coat hide his sword. "We cannot trust that anyone is who they appear to be. From now on, every citizen of this town is a potential enemy and we will treat them as such."

He looked around, but nobody argued.

They moved past dark, quiet stalls, and Saracen navigated them unerringly through the narrow gaps between buildings until he came to a stop, and grunted.

"The Gate is three streets away," he said, keeping his voice down. "But, beyond that corner ahead, people are standing in the dark. They are waiting for us."

"How many?" asked Ravel.

"Two, perhaps three hundred."

Nobody spoke for a moment.

"That is a lot of people," said Dexter.

Saracen nodded. "The only way we could get through without encountering the enemy would be to contact Tome and have him teleport us straight to the Gate."

"We cannot teleport in," said Hopeless. "They most assuredly have sigils guarding against Teleporters carved into the walls closer to the Gate."

"You can fly," Rapture said to Valkyrie. "Could you take us over their heads?"

"One or two at a time, maybe," Valkyrie said, "but I light up when I'm in the air. I'm not exactly subtle."

"We do not want you flying," said Skulduggery. "Strickent does not know you have come after him. You are the only advantage we have, and we do not want to lose that. Sister Zeal, it appears as though we will be requiring your services." He pulled the gag from her mouth. "You are going to walk us right by your fellow believers. We shall keep our heads down, but, if anyone asks, we have been converted, too. We are all one big happy family."

Zeal smiled. "And why should I help you?"

"Because we will kill you if you do not," he told her. "Does the Hidden God provide an afterlife?"

"He does," Zeal said after a slight hesitation. "Those who die in service to him will be granted eternal life in his paradise."

"The paradise beyond that portal, you mean? The one you were so desperate to leave?"

Her lip curled. "My Lord will grant me untold power when I die, you pathetic creature. Once I have proven myself worthy, I will know an eternity of strength and I will command legions."

"Once you've proven yourself worthy," Skulduggery said. "Which you have not done yet. So, if you die now, what happens to you? Your soul flits into his universe like a beautiful moth, but instead of power and authority you get an eternity of your wings being pulled off?"

She glared at him and said nothing.

Skulduggery nodded. "You do not want to die tonight, Zeal. You want to live so that you will have a chance to prove yourself. The only way you get to live is if you do what we tell you."

"You realise that if I take you to Strickent Abhor, he will kill you all?"

"You let us worry about that."

She smiled. "Then we have an agreement."

"We cannot trust her," Rapture said.

"She might betray us before we reach the Gate," Skulduggery agreed, holding his knife to Zeal's ribs while Ravel removed her shackles. "In which case, she will be the first to die. If we have to fight two hundred people, then we shall draw them to us, try to manage how many we fight at any one time. We will fall back to here, where we can corral them into a straight line and we need only defend from in front. Once we know we're going to be overwhelmed, we will take to the rooftops and move east. Does anyone have any objections?"

Nobody did.

"Then that is the plan," Skulduggery said, taking Zeal by the arm and leading the way forward.

They emerged on to a wider street, and now Ghastly could see the men and women – Strickent's new converts – assembled ahead. Their low conversation dried up and Zeal tried to walk through them, but they refused to part. She took a moment.

"Move aside," she said very, very slowly.

The man in front looked at them warily. His eyes were the eyes he'd been born with, not the startling blue of Zeal's or Strickent's. "I don't recognise your face, woman. I don't recognise the faces of your companions – those whose faces I can even see. Why do these two wear their hoods?"

"Because of the rain," Zeal said.

"It is not raining."

"You hear the thunder, do you not? The rain is coming."

"Are your companions so afraid of getting wet?"

Zeal pressed her hand against the man's face and energy burst from her palm and flung him backwards into the crowd, dead long before his body crumpled to the ground.

"You are all my brothers and sisters," Zeal announced. "You all share my love for the Hidden God. But look at me. Look at my eyes. I was not gifted my magic upon conversion – my magic is my own, and I am using it in service of the Hidden God. My eyes mark me as one of his chosen – and you would stand in my way? You would obstruct my path?"

No one said anything until a woman squared her shoulders. "We don't know you."

"I am Zeal, second only to Strickent Abhor. The enemy took me, held me prisoner. These people aided me in my escape and now I bring them to our Lord so that they, too, can be converted. That is who I am. Now who are you?"

The woman cleared her throat. "I am—"

"Nobody," Zeal interrupted. "You are nobody. But that is nothing to be ashamed of. You are but a grain of sand in a desert, yet without those grains of sand, there is no desert. I appreciate you. I love you. But stand aside, all of you, or Strickent Abhor will hear of this outrage."

Mumblings passed through the crowd and then it parted, wide enough for two to fit through at a time. Skulduggery and Zeal went first. The others followed. Ghastly began counting the rest of his life in streets crossed and corners rounded. With each waypost they passed, the tension grew. The crowd was silent, their frowns heavier the closer they stood to the green courtyard.

The Dead Men and their companions travelled along the tunnel of townspeople, suspicious and unsure, and Mevolent's own soldiers, recently converted to the ways of the Hidden God, and then the tunnel became one of stone where the dark night darkened further. A flash of lightning lit up the curvature of cloud-filled sky ahead of them, and thunder reverberated down through the walls to shake beneath their feet. When they emerged into the courtyard, Strickent Abhor turned to them, half of his features lit up by the light from the portal. The Unix Blade hung from his belt.

"Zeal," he said, "you have returned to us."

"And I have brought guests," Zeal said as Skulduggery moved his knife up to her throat.

"Strickent," Skulduggery said, "I do not imagine you will surrender to us, will you?"

Strickent smiled. "Surrender, when I have hundreds of acolytes within shouting distance? I think not. But I admit – you have caught me by surprise, Skulduggery. Are you not too busy to be bothering with the likes of us? Are the bedraggled remnants of your army not being slaughtered by Mevolent's forces as we speak? These are the reports I have been hearing. It is a rout, they say. It is indecent. How many did Meritorious bring, do you mind me asking? The overwhelming majority of your numbers? And then he placed them all in a camp like little lambs awaiting the axe? And yet you are here, the legendary Dead Men, running from the battle like scared children."

"We have our priorities."

"A silly portal takes priority over your fellow sorcerers?"

"Why not tell us what it is and where it leads, and let us decide where our attention should be focused?"

Strickent's smile grew. "You are trying to trick me."

"He is," said Zeal.

"Hush, madam," Skulduggery said, pressing the tip of the blade deeper into her throat.

Zeal laughed. "Kill me, then. The Hidden God will see my sacrifice and reward me in eternity. They know about you, Abhor. They have Valkyrie Cain with them."

Skulduggery grunted in annoyance, positioning Zeal slightly in front of him, like a shield.

Strickent's smile faltered as Valkyrie stepped up, tapping the metal skull, letting that wonderful suit flow over her.

"Detective Cain," he said, sounding aggrieved. "You are unusually persistent, are you not?"

"Abhor, come on," she responded. "This is hardly my fault. We can't very well have you wandering through time, making a general nuisance of yourself, now can we? It's just not on, dude."

"The Hidden God told me they would send someone to try to stop me. The Hidden God also told me that whoever they sent would fail."

"It sounds like the Hidden God told you what he felt he needed to tell you," Valkyrie responded. "The fact is, I smacked you around the place in the twenty-first century, and I'll smack you around the place in the eighteenth if you don't cop on to yourself."

Strickent's smile returned. "But I was a different person then, full of weakness and doubts. Look at me, Detective. Am I not better in every way?"

"You've got a glow in your cheeks, I'll give you that – but that might just be those fancy tattoos. Don't worry, I'll see what I can do about smacking them off you while I'm kicking your ass."

"I just love how confident you are," Strickent said, chuckling. "But you've made one tactical error, I'm sorry to say. Coming to me here, where I can pull power straight from the portal? You're simply not strong enough to stop me. None of you are. I'm afraid I'm going to have to kill all of you. Although... I don't know. Maybe I'll send you to meet the Hidden God, Detective Cain. Maybe he would convert you, if he found you worthy."

"Is he in there?" Valkyrie asked. "If he's standing on the other side, then sure, I'll pop in, say hi."

Strickent pursed his lips, then shook his head. "On second thoughts, perhaps not. You have a habit of killing gods, don't you?"

Valkyrie sighed. "You kill one god one time and suddenly you're a god-killer. You kill a bunch of them and suddenly no one wants to play any more. What's he like, though? How tall is he? He's shorter than you'd think, isn't he?"

"The Hidden God is not bound by flesh as we are, Detective. He watches us without eyes, speaks to us without lips, and guides us without hands."

"So he's pretty odd-looking, is what you're saying."

Zeal suddenly twisted, wrenching herself free from Skulduggery. "They want your knife!" she called. "They want to use it to kill the old man!"

"You are quite the chatterbox tonight, aren't you?" Skulduggery said, but didn't move to grab her back.

Strickent's eyes flickered past Ghastly to Shudder and, standing beside him, Tithonus.

"Ah, you think that will work, do you?" he asked with a laugh, taking the Unix Blade from its sheath and letting the light from the portal glint off it. "Let me save you some effort: it won't. Plunge this into the old man's heart, into his head, and you will hurt him, you will make him scream and bleed, but you won't kill him. Killing him is beyond you."

"They plan to kill him twice," said Zeal. "Kill him now, and again in the future."

The smile left Strickent's lips, and Ghastly knew, in that instant, that Skulduggery's plan would work.

"Hold on," said Zeal, frowning at Ghastly and his companions. "One of them is missing."

"What?" said Strickent.

"The Dead Men," she said. "There are only six."

Before Strickent could begin to count, he vanished, enveloped by a wall of empty space, and Zeal lunged to help, but Skulduggery pushed at the air and she smacked her head against the wall behind and crumpled. As quickly as he had vanished, however, Strickent returned, the invisibility bubble collapsing as he stood with one hand closed round Hopeless's throat, the other crushing the cloaking sphere. The Unix Blade lay on the grass at their feet, and Hopeless thrust the knife Meritorious had given him towards Strickent's throat. But Strickent caught his hand and wrenched the weapon from his grip.

"Nice try," Strickent said to Hopeless, and drove the knife deep into his heart.

After that, hell broke loose.

21

Rain started to fall as the converts came through the tunnel, a roaring mass of fury and violence, and the Dead Men crashed into them. The converts' faces were the faces of mortals, but their eyes burned with new hatred. Their hands were the hands of farm workers and stall owners, men who poured beer and women who washed floors, but their fingers curled and crackled with new power. The Hidden God had worked his way inside them and they were his now. Ghastly would have loved to treat them gently, and if he thought they might be rescued after this, might be returned to normal, perhaps he would have tempered his blows. But in battle, like in life, harsh moments must be met with equal if not greater harshness. It was the only way to win. It was the only way to survive. Hopeless had known that, but he was dead now, and not even that knowledge had been enough to save him.

A stream of energy burst from a merchant's hand, almost blindingly bright in the darkness, but he was jostled by a fellow convert and the stream missed Ghastly, but Ghastly didn't miss him. His axe took half the merchant's foot and then he shoved him to one side. A knife swiped at his shirt, running cold along his ribs, and Ghastly crunched the back of his axe into a face. The air rippled – it was impossible to say if it had been Skulduggery or Ravel who did it – and converts went flying, and Dexter blasted a woman, just enough to give himself some room, and lightning flashed as he stabbed her with his sword.

The converts were unused to magic. They'd been gifted with a miracle and were determined to use it, despite panic and confusion scrambling their ability to wield it properly. The thing about axes, Ghastly had always found, was that it mattered not how confused or frightened you were upon the swing of it – the axe was still an axe and, when it found a skull to cleave in two, it did not falter in its objective.

The rain fell harder, making it difficult to see, and the Dead Men hacked and slashed and cleaved, using magic only when they had to. Rapture's sword had been blunted by all the blood-letting, so she took a new one from the hand of a man she'd just killed and set about killing another.

Ghastly avoided a spear to the throat by pure luck. He grabbed the spear, snarling at the man who held it, and swung his axe, but it didn't go deep enough. They staggered around like this, locked together, while Saracen slashed and cut and Dexter helped Shudder against three old women armed with knives. They were vicious, those old women. They howled and screeched like they belonged in a jungle somewhere.

Ghastly disentangled himself and this time, when he swung the axe, it went in deep. His opponent fell and Ghastly let the axe go with him as Ravel ran by, clicking his tongue. Ghastly brought his hands in, the air rippling as it lifted Ravel high overhead.

Ravel landed, scattering the enemy, and before they could recover he was moving, blades flashing. Not one of them managed to even swing a sword – but then a spear went through Ravel's leg and he fell.

The rest of the Dead Men immediately rushed to his aid. The converts, sensing some semblance of a victory, redoubled their efforts. Rapture tore into them. Ghastly slipped in the mud, went down in a jumble of angry, hissing faces, scraping fingers and heavy elbows. He fought until there was such a tangle on top of him that he couldn't move his arms, when all he could manage was to raise his head.

Valkyrie collided with Strickent. Blue energy poured from his hand, but she dodged it, grabbed his wrist, snapped his elbow and broke his knee. They had healed again by the time he'd even stumbled.

The sheer numbers coming through that tunnel forced the Dead Men away from Ravel. A soldier kicked the sword from his hand, went to stab downwards, but Skulduggery managed to get there in time. The soldier switched targets without hesitation. A swipe, a thrust, a stab: these were the things Skulduggery shrugged off, and then their blades locked and Skulduggery twisted and the soldier's sword was torn from his grip. Skulduggery roared and the soldier held up his hands and Skulduggery's sword took those hands at the wrists even as it took his head from the shoulders.

Ghastly hissed as he got to his feet at last, searched through the lashing rain for a weapon, picked up a broken sword and killed someone with it.

A knife plunged into Ravel's shoulder and Skulduggery sprang over him, whirling, twirling, his sword flying. Tall soldiers were felled like trees and small soldiers chopped like logs. Swords hacked at him in response, cutting through his leathers, cutting through to bone, and Skulduggery screamed with each blow, but didn't stop, didn't slow, didn't even acknowledge the pain. He stabbed his sword through a breastplate and left it there, seizing an axe and deflecting a spear. The axe turned the spear to splinters, and a graceless spin was all it took to turn the skull of the spear-wielder to splinters, too. The air rippled and the axe shot from Skulduggery's hands, cleaving a path through the soldiers.

Skulduggery stood over the injured Ravel, meeting the enemy unarmed. He cracked arms, snapped knees, broke jaws, smashed ribs, but the enemy kept coming, slipping and sliding and muddied and bloodied, and they were swarming him now, grabbing him, pinning his arms, pinning his legs, all around him, blocking him from sight. Saracen and Dexter and Shudder and Rapture tried hacking a path to them. Ghastly barrelled by someone, elbowed someone else, making his way across a ground tangled with bodies to the mob of soldiers pulling Skulduggery apart. Lost in the middle of that maelstrom, Skulduggery was screaming, his screams becoming something unearthly, something inhuman, something unrecognisable.

Ghastly screamed, too, roaring commands that nobody listened to, that nobody even heard over the rain and the thunder and the battle. He screamed at the converts to get away, to leave his friends alone, to leave them be. The maelstrom continued and the screams changed and Ghastly faltered as spears of shadow lanced through the bodies of the dozens of soldiers who had piled on top of Skulduggery, taking them upwards, holding them in mid-air with Skulduggery below them at their centre. His leathers in ragged trails, darkness curling round his skeleton, turning the white bone to black, he raised his head to the gurgling, dying soldiers that he was keeping aloft.

One by one the soldiers died, went limp on those dark spikes, and more ran in, yelling war cries like that was going to do them any good.

The spikes retracted and the dead soldiers fell, and Skulduggery turned to greet the onrushing enemy. Before they reached him, a sword formed in his fist, a sword of pure shadow, and Skulduggery cut a swathe through the fools who seemed so eager to embrace death.

Ravel got to his feet, a knife in his hands, and went to defend Skulduggery against a soldier running up behind him. But Skulduggery whirled, swiping his sword through Ravel to get at the soldier beyond, cutting them both in half, and then turning back to continue his carnage.

Valkyrie grabbed Ghastly as he stumbled, her arm round his waist to stop him from falling.

"Skulduggery," he whispered.

"Vile," she said.

22

Skulduggery, or whoever the being was who now stood in his place, stepped over to the tunnel as the next wave of converts came screaming through and he flung out his arms and all those shadows turned sharp and thin and filled that tunnel, and the screaming stopped, went silent, replaced by a single agonised moan.

A part of Ghastly's mind detached itself from the rest of him and calculated how many people had just died. Over a hundred, without a doubt.

The shadows retracted and the dead people in the

tunnel crumpled against each other – some of them collapsing, some of them without even room to fall. The soldiers already in the courtyard – those with the startling blue eyes – were smart enough to give their enemy some room. They backed off, unsure, Zeal among them.

"Lord Vile," said Strickent, his face going slack for a moment before he laughed. "This is magnificent! This is astonishing! Skulduggery Pleasant is Lord Vile! How did I never know that? How was this ever kept a secret?"

"Lord Vile," Saracen said, barely audible, and shook his head. "How typical of Skulduggery's darker half to give itself a promotion."

The shadows gathered round Vile's waist and then grew tendrils that lifted him into the air, over the courtyard.

"You knew, though, didn't you?" Strickent asked Valkyrie, raising his voice to be heard over the rain. "You knew the Skeleton Detective was once the most feared of all of Mevolent's mass-murdering generals, and you were OK with it. You fought alongside one of the most evil killers on the planet, while you positioned yourselves as good-hearted heroes. I'd call you out as a loathsome hypocrite, Detective Cain, but of course you're not, are you? Because you're the same. Have you not partaken in the occasional slice of mass murder yourself? By the Hidden God, this is a tangled web you're weaving."

It was hard to know if Lord Vile had even heard most of what Strickent had said – his attention seemed to be on the shadows curling around the bones of his fingers – but at the mention of the Hidden God his head rose just a fraction, as if the name had managed to get through the darkness, to the person who had once been Skulduggery Pleasant. A sliver of shadow whipped out, but Strickent saw it coming and protected himself with a wide swathe of blue light.

"That is unfortunate," Strickent called to him. "I would have been prepared to let you leave, Lord Vile, to let you wreak whatever havoc you wanted upon the Sanctuaries or upon Mevolent or upon the mortals... I would have watched with amusement and applauded your efforts. But if you intend to make an enemy of me and, by extension, an enemy of the Hidden God, then I'm afraid I can no longer indulge your continued existence."

Strickent thrust his left hand into the blue, swirling

257

energy of the portal and held out his right. The energy passed through him and burst from his palm, the stream widening as it travelled so that when it smashed into Vile, scattering his shadows and incinerating the clothes beneath, it was wide enough to encompass his whole body.

The skeleton hung like that for a moment, lit up in the stark light, its spine arched, its fingers splayed, and then its bones disintegrated under the onslaught and Lord Vile was gone.

The soldiers cheered, shouting their triumph, praising the Hidden God, and Valkyrie roared in anguish and Strickent lowered his hands. Ghastly blinked the rain out of his eyes as his vision readjusted to the relative darkness, and he watched Vile's shadows twist as lightning stabbed the air, like falcons searching for their falconer.

"What an unexpected delight," Strickent said, smiling at Valkyrie as she stared upwards. "One less opponent to deal with when I return to our time. Do I kill you now, too, Detective Cain? Leave you as a pile of ash for the wind to pick up and scatter?"

"I'll kill you," Valkyrie said – promised – lowering

her eyes to him. Those eyes of hers, they crackled with energy, and she stalked forward, hands clenched into fists. Strickent's soldiers ran at her and she flung lightning of her own and they went spinning away, their flesh scorched, their cries loud.

"Wait," said Ghastly. "Valkyrie, stop."

There must have been something in his voice, something that conveyed his confusion, because she did, indeed, stop, and she looked back at him, and then looked up as Vile's shadows found each other and twisted together as they drifted to the ground.

A black skeleton touched down, a black skeleton made of solid shadows. It looked at its hand, opened and closed its fingers, discovering who it was all over again. Its head tilted, then turned towards Strickent.

At Zeal's command, soldiers charged and Lord Vile snapped out both hands and darkness flew from his fingertips, impaling the soldiers and stopping them before they'd travelled more than a few steps. The darkness retracted with only a few drops of blood spilled, and the soldiers crumpled. Vile walked towards Strickent.

Strickent once more plunged his left hand into the Gate and let the energy flow from his right. The beam hit Vile and scattered his shadows, but when it cut off again the shadows just flowed back together and the skeleton kept walking.

Zeal shouted a battle cry and leaped for him and Vile struck her, taking her off her feet. More of Strickent's soldiers ran in and a black sword formed in Vile's hand. He moved suddenly, cutting through the opposition with startling efficiency. A soldier lunged with a spear, but it was as if the spear passed through the memory of a ribcage, one that became real again once the danger had passed. In return, Vile cut the soldier in two. Diagonally.

Something passed over Strickent's face – annoyance, frustration, maybe even a hint of fear – and he turned to the Gate and raised his hands. The sigils on his skin burned brighter.

"He's widening the Gate!" Valkyrie shouted, running forward.

Some of the soldiers diverted from Vile, ran instead for Valkyrie, blocking her path. Saracen and Dexter plunged into their midst while Shudder's Gist screeched through them. Ghastly ducked an axe and broke a jaw, pulled the axe from the weakening grip and chopped at the neck proffered. A soldier with a spear ran in, but Rapture slipped by at the last moment, dropping to her knees and skidding past the soldier, her sword hacking at his shins. He squealed, started to stumble, and Ghastly's axe met his head.

More soldiers came in, blocking Rapture from sight. Ghastly lost his newly acquired axe and just started punching whoever was closest. Someone grabbed him around the waist, dragged him backwards, and they were on top of him, hitting him, stomping on him, and a knife sank into his side. He filled his hand with fire, pressed it into a face, and there was a scream and the hand holding the knife let go. Then a boot came in, caught him in the back of the head. Someone else was stabbing him in the leg. Ghastly bit an ear and gouged an eye.

Down here, on his back in a puddle of rainwater, he couldn't throw punches and he could barely cover up, so all of his mother's teachings meant little as he fought purely for the sake of fighting. He was going to die here, that was clear. He didn't mind that. He was too tired and in too much pain – with too many knives sticking out of him – to worry overly much about living any longer than he had to. *There is the fight,* his mother had once told him, *and nothing else.* If he'd had time to shrug, he'd have shrugged. So be it.

And then there was no one hitting him any more, no one stomping on him or trying to put new and different knives into him. He blinked as Dexter dragged a soldier off him, and Rapture grabbed his hands, pulled him to his feet.

"Are you all right?" she asked, the rain washing the blood down her face.

"No," he answered. "Are you?"

"Not remotely."

Shudder's Gist howled in protest as it was dragged back into his chest. Saracen kicked a soldier, making sure he was dead, and then sank to one knee, exhausted. Zeal tried to get to her hands and knees, but her clothes were drenched with rain and her own blood, and Ghastly reckoned she was too busy trying to keep breathing to offer up much of a challenge. The battle was over, save for Valkyrie and Strickent.

Valkyrie flew through the night sky, swooping low to throw lightning and then veering away to avoid Strickent's energy streams. He had moved from the portal to get a better angle so he was no longer channelling the power of his god's paradise but, even so, those streams were powerful enough to scorch through stone without stopping. One of them finally hit Valkyrie, and her suit, that wonderful suit, convulsed and flowed back to the metal skull and she hit the ground, grunting with the impact as she rolled. But, before Strickent could finish her off, the shadows coalesced behind him and Lord Vile stabbed him through the back.

Strickent gasped, held up on his toes, staring at the tip of the shadow sword protruding from his chest.

Vile slowly withdrew the sword and it disappeared into his hand like a river flowing into the sea, and Strickent staggered, dropping to his knees. Vile turned to the Gate, tilting his head, examining the energy up close, fascinated by it.

There was a chance. There was one chance left.

"Get Tithonus," Ghastly whispered to Rapture, then forced himself to move quicker, to move quieter. Holding his breath to stop the moans of pain, he hurried to the spot where Strickent had dropped the Unix Blade. He crouched, moving Hopeless's body out of the way. Beneath his friend, the knife. He picked it up, the light from the Gate catching on the sigil carved into the blade.

"Stop," Strickent said, too stunned by the blood leaking out of his chest to even try to stand.

Lord Vile turned, watching him, but not moving, as Ghastly backed away. Tithonus shuffled up to him, helped by Rapture and Shudder. Valkyrie limped over, tapping the metal skull. After a few attempts, her suit re-established itself, and she took the Unix Blade from Ghastly's hand.

"Stop," Strickent repeated. He took a deep breath before speaking again. "You don't know what you're doing."

Tithonus's wrinkled face was calm. "I am ready," he said.

Grunting with the effort, Strickent got to his feet. Vile didn't move to stop him.

"If you kill that man," said Strickent, "you'll die. Your world will die."

Valkyrie was too busy nursing her ribs to give a proper scowl, but she did her admirable best. "You think I want to do this? You really think I want to kill him?"

"They lied to you," Strickent said, his voice a little

stronger. The blood had stopped flowing from him and he was standing straighter. He was healing. "What did they say, the Elders? I assume they told you that you'd have to kill him twice, yes?"

"This is Skulduggery's plan."

Strickent glanced at Vile, who was still only standing there. "Then he lied to you. What did he say would happen?"

The rain began to ease.

"Tithonus is the anchor keeping you here," said Ghastly, "but when he dies you will be banished to the twenty-first century and the sorcerers there will have to deal with you."

"But that's not all," Strickent said. "Killing Tithonus with that knife will fix the timeline that I corrupted when I travelled back here. The world will be reset. How can you not see what this means? Everything that's happened since I arrived in this ridiculous time period will be wiped away. Skulduggery Pleasant was willing to sacrifice all of you to do this. He didn't tell you the truth because he knew what it meant. The people you are right now, in this moment, Ghastly Bespoke and Sister Rapture, Dexter Vex and Saracen Rue and Anton Shudder, will simply cease to be, as your entire world blinks out of existence. You will be replaced by different versions of yourselves. You, the people I see before me, will die."

Ghastly looked down at Hopeless, tried looking across at Ravel's remains, but they were covered by the bodies of the converts. A reset would bring his friends back. A reset would mean the townspcoplc had never been converted. A reset would mean Meritorious and Crow had never been killed. But a reset would wipe clean the last few days like blood from a wound.

He looked at Rapture. "We will not have met."

She looked back at him. "We will be killing ourselves."

"This world has taken a dark turn," said Shudder. "Replacing it would give it a chance at a better outcome."

Dexter and Saracen didn't say anything. Ghastly just kept looking at Rapture.

"This is ridiculous," said Strickent. "Simply ridiculous." He glared at Vile. "And you are going to let this happen? You are going to let them kill you, too?"

Lord Vile tilted his head at him, and then his shadows twisted and he vanished.

"You've lost, Abhor," said Valkyrie. "Once Tithonus dies, this will never have happened."

"Fine," Strickent snarled. "Kill him here, then. But I will not let you kill him twice."

He lunged for the Gate and Valkyrie dived after him and Ghastly prepared to fight, but, instead of using the power of the Hidden God's paradise to blast them, Abhor used it to vanish, and Valkyrie was left clutching awkwardly at nothing but air.

"Dammit," she said. "He's gone back."

"Back in time?" asked Rapture.

"Back to the future," said Valkyrie. "I can't delay. I've got to get to Tithonus before he does." She limped over to Tithonus, took him by the hand, and glanced at Ghastly. "How do you say *I'm sorry* in Italian?"

"*Mi dispiace.*"

She looked at Tithonus, deep into his eyes, and said, "*Mi dispiace.*"

"Do not be sorry," Tithonus answered in his own language. "My life never amounted to much. My death, at least, will help people and save lives. It is more than I could have ever hoped for."

Valkyrie clearly didn't understand anything beyond *dispiace*, but his tone was unmistakable, and she smiled sadly and nodded, gave his hand an extra squeeze. She

267

pressed the Unix Blade to his chest, but her hand was shaking, and Ghastly stepped forward.

"I will do it," he said.

"No. No, it should be me."

He took the knife from her. "It can be both. I shall kill him first; you kill him second."

She nodded, overwhelming gratitude brimming in her eyes, and Ghastly stepped up to Tithonus, who puffed his chest out as far as he was able.

"I've been ready for this since I first noticed that accursed Gate," he said, his eyes closed.

Rapture put her hand over Ghastly's, and he looked at her and she nodded to him.

The blade sank into Tithonus's chest and his eyes sprang open in a kind of amazement. His knees buckled and Ghastly caught him, laid him on the grass. As gently as he could, he removed the Unix Blade and straightened. Valkyrie took the knife, secured it inside her suit, fixed her hood and mask into place, and lowered her head. A moment later, she collapsed in on herself and disappeared.

Ghastly got ready to stop existing.

"What does this mean?" Rapture asked quietly,

keeping the rain from Tithonus's eyes. The old man managed a shaky smile. "If Valkyrie succeeds, should we not have already been replaced? Would it not have been instantaneous?"

"She's our friend," said Ghastly, "which means she has proved herself to our future selves, which means we trust her, which must mean she does not stop fighting until the job is done."

"I agree," said Dexter. "I do not know how time-travel works, but I have faith. You cannot fight alongside someone like that and not start to trust her."

"So we wait," said Rapture, and nodded. "Very well. I can trust in Valkyrie, as I trust in the Lady of Darkness."

Shudder came over, wincing in pain as he lowered himself to a seated position. "Did any of you manage it?" he asked. He slipped a hand into his shirt. When he brought it out, it was covered in blood. "All your talk about breaking free from an invisible structure, about seizing an opportunity for happiness to spite capricious fate. Do you remember? Reaching into the machinery of time and circumstance and making something new?"

"We remember," said Saracen.

"And did you manage to do any of it?"

Ghastly said nothing, but he stood, and took Rapture's hand and pulled her slowly to her feet. The rain had plastered a strand of hair across her cheek and he moved it with his fingers. He could have looked at her forever but, equally, the world could vanish in an eyeblink and so he cupped her face in his hand and kissed her softly and she kissed him back. Her arms went around his neck and thunder rumbled and his heart expanded in his chest. One hand was in her hair now and the other at the small of her back.

When they parted, he became aware of a kiss between Saracen and Dexter, and then movement behind them.

He pulled away from Rapture and snatched up a sword as Baron Vengeous dropped from the roof into the courtyard.

"What villains you are," Vengeous said. "Killing an innocent mortal to protect your own greater good? How disgraceful. How contemptible. As if your preferred outcome is the only one that matters. As if there are not those who would choose to stay in the version of the world where Meritorious and Crow are dead, where your army has just been slaughtered, where victory is within our grasp. We will heal the old man. We will keep him safe forever. We will learn to draw power from that portal and add it to our own."

Mevolent floated down from the dark sky and landed in front of them, his sword glinting. "And all of you," he said, "will die forgotten."

23

Valkyrie pulled her wet mask off her face, letting it disappear into the hood even as she yanked the hood down and grabbed her phone from the bedside table.

The same date she'd left from – in fact, only a few seconds had gone by since she'd been here last. But Skulduggery had been standing right there, watching her. Now the hotel room was empty. And different. Different-coloured walls, nicer sheets on the bed, the bed itself in a different position. The street outside the window was narrow and pretty and hadn't changed noticeably. The cars, though – the cars were sleeker. Quieter. She frowned, realising that her phone was different. Thinner.

Shoving it into her pocket, Valkyrie walked out of the room and left the hotel. Whatever havoc had been wreaked on the timeline, whatever changes had been made, they didn't appear to be affecting the people she passed. They chatted to each other, tapped on their phones, took their dogs for a walk in the afternoon sunshine, frowned at the fact that she appeared to have emerged fresh from a storm.

The air. Did the air smell different? It was clean, warm mountain air – but did it smell even cleaner than when she'd been here last?

She got to Tithonus's house, but a family was living there. They didn't speak English and she still couldn't speak Italian so she gave up trying to describe Tithonus and instead found a deserted alley where she could blast up to a roof without being seen. She searched for Tithonus's aura, eventually finding it to the south. She could have reached it in seconds by flying, but it was a clear day and she'd have been spotted immediately, so she returned to street level and walked quickly.

If Skulduggery had been here, they'd have driven there in the car he usually kept locked away in a garage in Naples specifically for adventures in Italy and Continental Europe: a black 1954 Maserati – a Berlinetta, Skulduggery called it. Number five out of only four that were ever made, however the hell that was possible. Valkyrie wondered if the car still existed.

She wondered if Skulduggery still existed.

At the corner ahead of her, two cops were standing in the shade, talking. She shoved Skulduggery out of her thoughts and did her best to appear casual. None of this would matter, anyway, once she did what she had to do. Then the timeline would straighten out and Skulduggery would come back. Easy. All she had to do was kill Tithonus.

Her guts twisted so much at the idea that she almost missed the fact that the cops talked even louder as she approached, like they were as busy as she was trying to appear casual. The moment she passed them, their conversation stopped, and she heard one of them say, "*Stregona.*"

Valkyrie didn't know what it meant, but she knew aggression when she heard it and when she glanced back they were already drawing their guns. Valkyrie cursed, folded her arms over her head and turned away as they opened fire, the bullets striking painfully against her shoulder blades and cracking into her spine and her wrist. She crouched, yanked up her hood and pulled down her mask, gritting her teeth as they moved up on either side of her, shooting into her torso, her legs, her head.

When they stopped to reload, she launched one of them over to the other side of the street with a flash of lightning and grabbed the other one, ripped the gun out of his hand and hit him with it until he fell.

Instead of running and screaming, instead of staring and recording all this on their phones, the people around her snarled, hatred in their eyes. They weren't astonished to witness the use of magic – they just despised her for it.

Valkyrie took off into the air.

24

Ghastly threw fire and lunged, but Vengeous ignored the flames that exploded harmlessly over his coat and parried Ghastly's sword with his cutlass, redirected his lunge so that Ghastly went stumbling over the corpses that littered the courtyard. Rapture jabbed with a spear, preventing Vengeous from skewering Ghastly through the back as he regained his footing on the wet grass, while Saracen and Dexter and Shudder focused their attention on Mevolent.

Every glimpse Ghastly caught of that battle made

him want to look away. The three Dead Men were tired and hurt, limping and bloodied, but they'd been in worse states and had fought on and Ghastly knew they were more than equal to the task were they facing any other opponent. But against Mevolent it was a different matter.

He was a giant of a man, but he moved like a dancer. His arms were slender, no great slabs of muscle in his chest, either, and yet every swing of that ridiculous sword could cleave a tree in two.

And that sword... It should have been impossible to wield, impossible to balance, and yet he flicked it out as if it was a knife, controlling it – one-handed sometimes – like it was a twig in the hands of a child.

Ghastly ducked a swipe of the cutlass and rammed his shoulder into Vengeous. Now it was Ghastly's turn to swipe, but his sword failed to cut through that fancy coat, and Vengeous snarled behind his grey-as-stone beard, blocked the next swing and caught Ghastly in the ribs with his left fist. It wasn't the hardest Ghastly had been hit in his life – not even the hardest he'd been hit tonight – but it landed perfectly and caved in a rib Ghastly badly needed to stay upright.

Wincing, reeling in a half-crouch, he watched Vengeous

bat Rapture's spear out of her hands, watched as she slipped by him, watched as he caught her with an elbow that sent her spinning.

Ghastly dropped the dulled sword and used the air to bring an axe into his hands.

25

Her hair whipping in the wind, Valkyrie found Tithonus's aura again and, once she was close enough, realised he was below ground – beneath the police station.

Growling, she swooped down, blasting open the station doors. She flew in, landed in a run, cracked an elbow into the jaw of the first cop she saw. People were shouting and alarms were going off and Valkyrie ignored them all, used her black lightning to turn the floor to dust and then she dropped down. It took a few goes, a few wrong turns, but eventually she landed in Tithonus's cell.

It wasn't just a cell, though. It had been converted into a permanent residence, albeit not a very nice one. A small TV played in the corner, and Tithonus, well past the halfway mark of his fourth century, gaped at her through all that dust.

"*Che costa sta succedendo?*" he said in a voice that barely rose above a whisper.

"Haven't a clue what you're saying," Valkyrie responded, walking over to where he sat in his wheelchair. "Can you speak English? You used to be able to speak English."

"I can speak English," said Tithonus.

"My name is Valkyrie Cain. Do you remember meeting me?"

"I'm sorry, my memory is not what it once was."

"Do you remember a man called Strickent Abhor? Do you remember the Gate to Hell?"

His impossibly ancient face soured. "I remember the Gate. I remember it ruining my life."

"But you don't remember Abhor, or Mevolent?"

"I remember Mevolent," said Tithonus. "Everyone remembers Mevolent."

She could hear shouts over the alarms, coming closer.

"I'm very sorry about this," she said, scooping one arm under his withered legs and the other behind his back. "*Mi dispiace.*"

She picked him up and it was like lifting something hollow, something brittle, and she flew upwards, through the holes she'd made in the ceilings, doing her best not to electrocute the old man as she made her escape through the dust and smoke and gunfire.

Once outside, she flew east.

26

The cutlass whispered coldly across Ghastly's belly and he fell to his knees in the mud. That was it, then. That was the end. Ghastly had encountered moments before and had thought them grave enough to be the end, but they were mere rehearsals for the real thing. This, finally, was the real thing.

His axe fell from numb fingers. Rapture lay nearby, hands at her neck, trying to stop the blood from leaving her body. He wanted, more than anything, to be with her. To help her. Almost more than anything. What he really wanted more than anything was to pick up his axe and take the head of Baron Vengeous, then stride over to the other side of the courtyard and take the head of Mevolent. Once that was done, he wanted to hold Rapture in his arms and get her to a healer, then live the rest of his life never having to hurt anyone ever again.

But the things Ghastly wanted and the things Ghastly got were rarely the same, and so all he could do was watch as Mevolent kicked Shudder away and avoided one of Dexter's energy streams and then spun, that ridiculous sword of his lopping Saracen's right hand off at the wrist.

Saracen staggered, yelling in shock but not yet pain, and tripped over a corpse's leg and fell. Mevolent stalked after him, swirling the sword over his head. It swung high and Mevolent prepared to bring it down, but Shudder roared and his Gist burst, shrieking, from his chest. It flew at Mevolent, fuelled by a lifetime of fury. Its claws raked his face, turning his cheek to bloody ribbons. It flew up and around, trailing its stream of light, and launched itself back at its enemy, mouth stretching wide and all those teeth on show. Mevolent twisted, and all those teeth and the claws skimmed by him, and he brought his sword down and severed the stream and the Gist vanished with a look of surprise on its twisted face. Shudder dropped to his knees, his shoulders slumped, his features blank.

Dexter Vex leaped on to Mevolent from behind, but Mevolent raised his free arm in time and Dexter's knife went through his hand rather than his throat. Ignoring the blade, Mevolent gestured and Dexter jerked away from him, struggling against the air itself. Energy gathered in his right hand, but his fingers twisted and bent and folded, and he screamed as his whole hand ruptured, and Mevolent poked him with that ridiculous sword and the sword went all the way through. Dexter stopped screaming and hung there until Mevolent dropped him.

27

Tithonus shielded his eyes from the sun. "Please," he whispered, "please don't take me beyond the town. The pain—"

"I won't, don't worry," Valkyrie said, spying a rooftop that was shielded from view. They landed, and she sat Tithonus against the low lip that ran round the edge of the building, then crouched before him and took down her hood.

"I'm sorry," she said. "I'm sorry about all of that. Would you like me to move you into the shade?"

"No," he said at once, blinking madly. "I haven't seen the sun for eight years. It is very bright."

"Tithonus, this is going to sound very hard to believe, but I've travelled in time."

"OK," Tithonus said.

She had to smile. "You don't find that weird?"

"*Sì*, I do," said Tithonus, "but I find many things about sorcerers to be weird. Time-travel is just one more. Do we know each other?"

"In a way. I travelled back to 1703 to stop a man called Strickent Abhor from opening the Gate to Hell. I failed, and a lot of people died – a lot of my friends."

Tithonus nodded. "Yes, yes, the Massacre at San Gimignano. This is a very famous battle. Thousands of sorcerers were killed just beyond the walls."

"Then I get back here and, somehow, the world has ended up like this and I don't know how."

"I suppose it... it *did* all start from that point, yes. I will try to explain this well." He frowned, thinking about it. "*Bene, sì.* The Massacre at San Gimignano led to Mevolent preparing to attack the mortal governments all around the world, but the Necromancers stopped him."

"The Necromancers?"

"Mevolent won the war against the Sanctuaries, yes? But the Necromancers won the war against Mevolent."

"And that's how this world ended up like this? The Necromancers are in charge?"

"No, no. After that came the Necromancer War, when the Necromancers fought each other. By then, though, the mortal governments were aware that magic existed, and they started their own war against them, although they kept it from public view. Many sorcerers were captured, many more killed. The captured sorcerers became *schiavi*. They provide energy and technology and they're used for healing and agriculture."

"What do you mean *used for*?"

"They are *schiavi*. Ah, I'm sorry. Slaves. They are slaves."

Valkyrie sat back. "Sorcerers are slaves? And people are OK with that?"

"Very few people knew about it," Tithonus said with a shake of his head. "Only governments, in fact. Then, twenty-two years ago, the sorcerers revolted. They broke free, all around the world, all at the same time. Suddenly everyone knows. Everyone can see magic."

"And what happened?"

An unhappy shrug. "The rebellion failed. The rebel leaders were killed as punishment. The rest went back to being slaves, but mortal people hated them because of the *spargimento di sangue*. The, ah, the bloodshed. They hate them still."

"Huh," said Valkyrie.

"This world is different from the one you know?"

"It is. In my version, mortals have no idea about magic."

"But I am still alive, am I?"

"You are."

Tithonus uttered what Valkyrie guessed was a long string of Italian obscenities. "Such is my curse. The song of the cicadas is the song I sing. No matter what happens, I do not die."

"That might not be strictly true."

His face went slack. "*Scusi?*"

She pulled the Unix Blade from her suit, laid it on the roof beside him. "This will kill you. I think. It's complicated, but you've already been killed with this in the past, in 1703. Or you should be, by now. If I... if I kill you with this, here, you should actually die."

"Impossible. Nothing can kill me. I am... Nothing can..." Tears rolled down his cheeks. "You could really do that? You could give me peace?"

"I think so."

"I cannot leave, you see. This town. I cannot leave this town. But you know this." He laughed. "Of course you know this. You know me. I cannot leave this town and I get older and older, but I cannot die. The people, everybody, they believe I am *stregone*, I am a sorcerer, even though they detect no magic. So they put me in a police cell and give me a television and some books and they feed me and... My life is a misery. I want peace. I am old and I have been cheated of my death. Please end my suffering."

"Tithonus, I... I'll be honest with you. I don't know if I can do it."

Tithonus's gaze flickered behind Valkyrie. "Then perhaps he could."

Valkyrie turned to face Strickent Abhor.

28

Ghastly held what had once been a spear, but was now a length of useless wood. Even the end that had snapped hadn't broken in such a way as to leave a sharp point for poking, for gouging, for stabbing or staking. It was slightly jagged, the kind of thing to give you splinters. He wondered if Vengeous was scared of splinters.

"Are you scared of splinters?" he asked him, words coming out in a jumble.

"What was that?" Vengeous responded, wiping the blood from his cutlass.

Ghastly swirled his thick tongue in his stupid mouth, and tried again. "Are you scared of splinters?"

Vengeous smiled. "No."

Damn. That had been Ghastly's only chance at winning this fight.

Stepping over a hacked-up corpse, he stumbled, nearly twisting his ankle. That would never do. Twisted ankles were awful. He could handle broken ribs and blood leaking out of him and knives sticking from his flesh, but twisted ankles were the worst. They were sore.

He wondered how much blood he had actually lost. He wondered if it was affecting him in any way. He wondered if he'd notice if the blood loss and the pain and the shock at losing his friends made him delirious. He decided that he needed to keep an eye out for delirium. Delirium in the middle of a battle was almost as bad as a twisted ankle.

Across the courtyard, Saracen Rue had one hand and a broken sword and he faced Mevolent alone.

On the ground behind Vengeous, Rapture still held one hand to her neck. The other hand was starting to crackle with energy, and she was holding it out, doing her best to aim. Ghastly prepared himself, gathering his strength to make one last dash. The stream that flowed from Rapture's hand wasn't strong and it faltered as soon as it hit Vengeous in the shoulder, but it made him stagger a little and Ghastly tried to bolt, but his first step plunged his foot into the ruined torso of a dead body and it stuck there as Vengeous turned slowly to Rapture. He strode over a carpet of corpses, pulling back the cutlass to stab down, and Ghastly dropped the broken spear, swept his hands up, and the air rippled around him and he was suddenly an arrow, miraculously on target.

He collided with Vengeous and they stumbled. Vengeous tried to shake him off, tried to disentangle, to give himself room to swing, and Ghastly didn't have any choice but to stay as close to him as possible. While he was there, he went to work, ignoring the aches and the pains as his fists crunched into flesh.

Vengeous grunted and fell back and Ghastly stayed with him. The cutlass slashed his leg, but Ghastly ignored it. He shifted targets, rattled out three straight jabs that destroyed Vengeous's nose, stepped in with a kidney shot, followed by a left to the ribs and then an uppercut that knocked Vengeous on to his back. As Vengeous sprawled, he snarled, his eyes narrowing. Ghastly had seen this before – he'd seen Vengeous's opponents explode – and he clicked his fingers and flicked out a fireball. It wasn't big and it wasn't on target, but it was enough to make Vengeous jerk away and then Ghastly dived on top of him. He pressed down on Vengeous's cheek with one hand, keeping his face turned away from him, and hit him with the other, all the while closing his own eyes against those desperate, scrabbling fingers.

He brought his knees in, bit by bit, on either side of Vengeous, and when he could he heaved himself upright and threw more punches, aiming for the beard. Vengeous covered up as best he could, but Ghastly caught him with one shot that sent a glaze over his eyes, and suddenly Ghastly had the energy of ten men and he finished him with a flurry, punching him into oblivion.

When he was done, he fell to one side, looking over at Saracen, realising he'd missed his friend's death.

29

"How did you do it?" Strickent asked. "How did you find him before I did? I even had a head start on you. You know something? I don't even want to know. I have a feeling it would annoy me. Hello, Tithonus. I'm not going to lie to you – you look awful. Now, I don't know what she's been saying, but I'm here to save you, OK? She wants to kill you, and I'm here to protect you."

"I want to die," said Tithonus.

Strickent rolled his eyes. "The one time I want to save a life and look what happens."

"You've got to let me do this, Strickent," said Valkyrie. "Have you looked around? Have you seen what kind of world this is? We've got to get our world back."

"Actually," Strickent said, "I kind of like this one. Fewer mages means less opposition."

"The mortals here are used to dealing with people like us. They'll have weapons we know nothing about."

"And I have a god they know nothing about. I'll take my god over their weapons any day. Detective Cain – Valkyrie – you don't have to kill him."

"She won't be," said Tithonus, and Valkyrie looked round as he plunged the Unix Blade into his own neck.

Strickent hollered and lunged past her and Valkyrie blasted him off the rooftop and fell to her knees beside Tithonus. With his last bit of strength, he pulled the knife out, and dropped it. Instinctively, Valkyrie's hands went to the wound to apply pressure.

"No, no," he said, smiling weakly, "you forget what you are meant to do, yes? I am supposed to die now. Let me."

She hesitated, then took her hands away. "I'm sorry," she whispered.

"I'm not," he replied, and said something in Italian. It sounded pretty.

He breathed out one last time as Strickent landed beside her and kicked Valkyrie in the side so hard she went spinning across the rooftop.

30

Mevolent stepped over Saracen's body and Ghastly tried to get up, but couldn't. He managed a single roll, though, before even the strength for that followed the flow of blood out of his system. Next to him, Tithonus barely breathed. Ghastly reached back, stretching for Rapture.

She reached for him at the same time but was too weak to shift closer. Their fingers almost touched.

"No matter what happens," he told her, his voice a dry whisper, "I'll find you."

Tithonus breathed out one final time just as Mevolent reached them and

31

"What have you done?" Strickent screamed.

Fresh memories rushing into her mind, jostling for space beside the ones already there, Valkyrie rose into a crouch, energy crackling. The world had changed, shifted in an unnoticeable instant. Tithonus was gone and Strickent's sigils had dimmed. They slowed in their movement, gradually coming to a stop on his skin as he lost his connection to the source of all that power.

She raised a hand, ready to fire. "Hey, Strickent," she said, with no idea where that sentence was going, but pretty sure it'd be somewhere cool, when a light flashed and something punched her in the back. She sprawled, her necronaut suit fleeing back into the metal skull. She tore up her elbows and knees on the rooftop and then turned over, groaning when she saw who'd attacked her.

"What the hell are you doing here?"

Zeal smiled as she hovered overhead. "The Hidden God deigned me worthy to survive for all these years, and my memories fit to keep," she said. "You have no idea of the discipline it took not to kill you as a newborn, Valkyrie Cain. I should be commended for my self-control."

Valkyrie groaned as she got back to her feet. "Yeah," she said. "Well done you for not killing a baby, you goddamn psycho." She tapped the skull and nothing happened.

"Brother Strickent," said Zeal, "I have been waiting for you for such a long time. We have much to talk about."

"We should kill her before we go," Strickent replied, glaring at Valkyrie.

"We have great things ahead of us, Brother. Great things. But we do not have time for pettiness."

She held out a hand. Strickent hesitated, then took it, and Valkyrie watched them rise up into the clear blue sky.

She didn't try to stop them.

Instead, she took out her phone. It was her normal phone, the phone she'd had right before she travelled back. She activated the locator and lay there, eyes closed, feeling the warmth of the sun. She was used to parallel timelines, having for years absorbed her reflection's memories at the end of every day, and she sorted through the new ones with something approaching – though not quite reaching – ease.

She found herself muttering softly, like she used to do sometimes as a teenager, as she pieced things together. Reality had managed to smooth over the cracks in the timeline, establishing a brand-new sequence of events that were as real to her as the events she had personally experienced. A headache had started somewhere behind her eyes, about which she wasn't the least bit surprised.

She heard a car pull up on the street below and, groaning a bit with the effort, walked to the edge of the building and dropped off the side. Cushioning her descent, she landed in someone's back garden and made her way to the street outside.

She tapped the skull and her suit flowed over her clothes, instinctively adopting a more casual style. It knew the fighting was over.

She walked out on to the pavement. Skulduggery stood beside the Berlinetta, wearing the same suit he'd been in the last time she'd seen him a week/just a few minutes ago. He had his phone pressed to his façade, and her phone started ringing. He heard her and turned, ended the call.

"You look like you've been in a fight," he said.

"More than one," she responded. "Where were you?"

"Waiting in the hotel room. Where were you?"

Valkyrie gave him a hug, then stepped back, squinting against the sun as she looked at him. "I returned to the hotel, but it was a different timeline and you weren't there. I've had to work a little to make sure you came back."

Skulduggery put his hat on Valkyrie's head, tilting the brim to shade her eyes. "You changed the timeline?"

"I fixed the timeline. I repaired the world."

"And Abhor?"

"Strickent Abhor is now covered in sigils and a lot

more powerful than he was when he left – so things didn't go exactly according to plan, but I think we both expected that."

"I would have been astonished if it had worked out any other way, quite frankly. Do you need to talk it through?"

"Naw," she said. "I'm good."

"OK then." He went to get in the car.

"Well," she said, "maybe just answer a few questions so I get things straight in my own head."

He turned back to her. "Of course."

"First of all," she said, "how's Tithonus?"

"Who's Tithonus?"

"He's the guy who discovered the Gate in 1583, but in this new timeline... ah, OK. Now the Gate was only discovered a few weeks ago – by Strickent Abhor."

Skulduggery nodded. "He was led to it by a voice in his head – the Hidden God, we assume. He tried to open the Gate—"

"But we foiled his plan," Valkyrie continued.

"And there was much in the way of banter and high jinks."

"We *are* hilarious."

"And just as we were about to put the shackles on, he told us if he couldn't open the Gate *now*, he'd just travel back to a time when there'd be no one to stop him – and he vanished.

"It took a few days to siphon some of the energy from Destrier's Plague Doctor suit into your Necronaut suit, by which time we'd figured out the most likely point that Strickent had jumped to was probably 1703."

Valkyrie raised an eyebrow at the way time, or the universe, or whatever, worked to fill in the gaps and made up the shortfalls as it restructured reality. "I might need a minute," she said. "I've got to tell you about two parallel timelines. In one of them, I hooked up with you and the Dead Men, and I'll tell you about that after. In the new timeline... let's see. When I arrived, Strickent already had the Gate open and he was already converted. Zeal was there, I'll tell you about her, too." There was a new memory that was so similar to an original, of Zeal plunging through the Gate for only a moment before being snatched back, now loyal to the Hidden God. It was an unsettling sensation, a feeling of *déjà vu* that Valkyrie knew was never going to fade. "I fought them both," she said, "Strickent and Zeal, and they kicked the crap out of me."

"Did they gloat about it?"

"They did!"

"Bad guys always do that."

"We sometimes do it, too."

"But when we do it, it's really funny."

She laughed. "Yeah, it is. And then Mevolent arrived."

His head tilted. "Mevolent?"

"Oh, Skulduggery, you have no idea. In the first timeline, we were going up against Mevolent and Vengeous and Serpine. It was huge. But the way things are now, it was just Mevolent. His Sensitives had picked up, like, this tremendous surge of energy and he was there to find out what it was. He actually helped me against Strickent and Zeal."

"You fought side by side?"

"He didn't know me, had no idea that we were enemies, so he didn't try to kill me, not even once. Which, I have to say, was weird. So Zeal was injured, and she got the hell out of there, and Strickent time-travelled again. Actually, I just met them both up on the roof there. Don't bother looking for them, they're gone."

"What about the Gate to Hell?" he asked.

"Mevolent sealed it and I came home."

"Did you speak before you parted ways?"

"Like, did we have a conversation? He asked me who I was."

"And what did you say?"

She shrugged. "I was all cool and mysterious, didn't say much."

"I see."

"But right before I came home?"

"Yes?"

"I gave him the finger."

"I'm so proud of you."

"Thought you would be."

"And what was the original timeline like?"

"It was interesting." She hesitated. "You killed Serpine."

His head tilted again. "I did?"

"You didn't mean to do it. He was our prisoner and you killed him. With shadow magic, no less."

"Necromancy? In 1703? How delightfully strange. I daresay my life would have turned out remarkably different if I'd had my revenge so early."

"Well, spoiler alert, it didn't work out too great for a lot of our friends."

"Oh," he said. "That does take some of the joy out of it, I have to admit."

They got in the Berlinetta and left the town behind them. Valkyrie pulled the hat low over her eyes, her exhaustion finally catching up with her. Before she nodded off, she mumbled, "I said *back to the future.*"

"I'm sorry?"

She raised the hat and looked at him, smiling weakly. "When I was in 1703, I said Strickent's gone *back to the future*, but there was no one there to catch my hilarious reference."

"What reference?"

"To the movie."

"What movie?"

She sighed. *"Back to the Future."*

"Never heard of it."

"I realise that you don't like to admit this, but you *have* seen popular movies, and I know for a fact that you've seen this one. We had an entire conversation about it when we were talking about the implications of time-travel. We talked about the paradoxes and the DeLorean and the Lone Pine Mall..."

Skulduggery let the façade flow from his skull. "We

did talk about time-travel films before you left, yes. We talked about *Somewhere in Time*, *Terminator 2* and *Looper*. We didn't talk about *Back to the Future* because I've never heard of that film and I've certainly never seen it."

"Are you serious?"

"Quite."

She sat up straighter and took off the hat. "Oh my God. We changed something."

"What do you mean?"

"When we went back," she said, speaking quickly, "either Strickent or I, we must have done something, interfered with the timestream in some way. I thought reality had been reset and all the cracks papered over, but this isn't the world I left. If *Back to the Future* doesn't exist, then what else has changed? People, events, advancements – oh, God. Oh, God, what have I done?"

"Oh, wait," Skulduggery said. "You mean Back *to the Future*? Oh, yes, I've seen that. I've seen them all. A great little trilogy."

He returned his attention to the road and she glared.

"I hate you," she said.